Catriona appealed to his better nature

"You wouldn't deliberately sh‗‗‗‗‗‗ld lady's illusions?" she aske‗‗‗‗‗‗ ‗ look of helpless appeal. She ‗‗‗‗‗‗ ‗ second later he smile‗‗‗‗‗‗

"I'll cooperate wit‗‗‗‗‗‗‗‗‗‗ he conceded light‗‗‗‗‗‗‗‗‗‗ ‗e for nuthin'' as t‗‗‗‗‗‗‗‗‗y—I'll play ball only if yo‗‗‗‗‗‗‗e."

"I don't understand‗‗‗‗‗‗d, perplexed. "All I'm asking you to do i‗ ‗ etend that we're friends."

"No," he said. "That doesn't fit in with my plans."

"*Your plans!*" she glared. "Your plans have nothing to do with me."

"The ball game, remember?" He smiled unpleasantly. "Far from wanting our mythical friendship dissolved, I've decided that it would suit me fine if it should blossom into an engagement."

Rapture of the Deep

Margaret Rome

Harlequin Books

TORONTO • NEW YORK • LOS ANGELES • LONDON
AMSTERDAM • PARIS • SYDNEY • HAMBURG
STOCKHOLM • ATHENS • TOKYO • MILAN

Original hardcover edition published in 1982
by Mills & Boon Limited

ISBN 0-373-02553-X

Harlequin Romance first edition June 1983

CHAPTER ONE

THE hush that had fallen over the darkly furnished book-crammed study occupied by the Head of the Department of Sciences in a noted Scottish university was redolent of shocked dismay. Catriona sat waiting with head bowed, studying the weave of her plaid skirt, fiercely determined to keep tears at bay.

'Why on earth are you doing this, girl?' Professor Sandwick's bushy eyebrows met in a frown when, after a second swift perusal of the letter she had placed upon his desk after he had left for home the previous evening, he sat back in his chair to concentrate his full, grave attention upon the slender, flaxen-haired girl with the quiet dignity of a Viking princess who had demonstrated from the first day of her arrival as an office junior a wealth of grit, tenacity and determination to succeed inherited from tough Shetland forebears. 'Did you seriously believe that after slinking into my study last night to deposit a letter of resignation on my desk you would not be called upon to offer a further, more comprehensive explanation? You have used the term "family commitments" to excuse your defection,' contemptuously he flicked a corner of her letter with a thumbnail, 'an expression often used not so many years ago by girls resigning because they were about to be married, or by married ladies anticipating the arrival of a baby. However, laws governing equal opportunities for women have disposed of the need for females to sacrifice their careers for the sake of *family commitments*, therefore if it is marriage you have in mind, Catriona, or even,' without a trace of compunction he shocked her bent head erect, 'if you should have suddenly discovered that you are pregnant, there is no need to over-react. Adequate leave can easily be arranged.'

She jumped to her feet, sparking a look of indignation at the Professor whom, in spite of an aloof, imperious attitude she had long since decided was cultivated specifically to keep rebellious students in order, she had always regarded as a friend, a father figure who, whenever he had sensed the homesickness that had often overwhelmed her during her first traumatic year of exile from her solitary island home, had ensured that so much work had been piled upon her desk that she had had little time to spare for feeling lonely or becoming prey to self-pity. The Professor of psychology had kept an experienced eye upon the sixteen-year-old junior whose isolated upbringing had made her too painfully shy to mix even with her own contemporaries and had prescribed and encouraged her to enrol upon a course of further education which, besides the obvious advantages to her career, had provided ample opportunity for her to become integrated into youthful society. His proud delight when eventually she had graduated from college having gained the highest distinction in the twin arts of shorthand and typing, commercial correspondence, office routine, English and two other languages had helped compensate a little for the absence of the parents she had never known.

'I strongly resent that suggestion, Professor!' she responded sharply, directing a glare of ice-green indignation across the width of his desk. 'During the years I've spent at this university I can't recall doing anything to justify your obviously low opinion of my morals. In fact,' to her chagrin her voice began to wobble, 'if I'd given the subject any thought, which needless to say I have not, I might have been inclined to favour the theory that a man such as yourself, a professor of psychology who's made a lifetime study of human and animal behaviour, wouldn't have much difficulty concluding that immorality is not one of my personal characteristics!'

'Just as I had imagined,' the Professor swiftly turned the tables. 'That any member of staff whose brilliance impressed her superior to such an extent that he did not hesitate to promote her from office junior to secretary to personal assistant, could believe that one sheet of paper containing a brief statement of intent would absolve her of the courtesy—no, dammit, the *duty*—of explaining to one who cares, to one who has striven in every way possible to help her achieve her ambitions, why she should suddenly and illogically have decided to abandon a promising career! I thought I'd become immune to the irresponsibility of modern youth,' his fist thumped down hard upon the surface of his desk, 'but this latest example of inconsistency has left me utterly appalled!'

'You surely don't imagine that I'm resigning from choice!' she cried out, prodded from her shell of reserve by the unjust accusation. 'Everything I've ever wanted from life is here in this university,' she stormed, oblivious to the fact that the Professor had relaxed in his chair, faintly smiling. 'I'm deeply aware of my good fortune, will never cease feeling grateful for the kindness and understanding you showed to a callow, lonely junior bewildered by the unfamiliar sights and sounds of a big city. I couldn't have gained half the diplomas I did without your help; thanks to you, I now have an interesting, well paid job situated conveniently close to Shetland and my one remaining relative! But now Aunt Hanna needs me, so I *must* return home,' she stressed, sea-green eyes dark with feeling. 'If you'd seen her as I did last week,' suddenly her voice dropped to a distressed whisper, 'body drooping with fatigue, hands furtively groping for items she obviously couldn't see; gnarled fingers stiff with rheumatism, and her dear brave face registering for the first time ever every one of her seventy-odd years, you would have realised as I did that she can't be left alone indefinitely.'

'Sit down, Catriona.' The deep, even tenor of his voice, his gentle glance and projected flow of sympathy were the first indications she received that she had been cleverly manipulated. She gaped, feeling suddenly foolish, then meekly capitulated.

'How dare you treat me like one of your patients!' she attempted a feeble jest, sinking down into a chair. 'I ought to have remembered that substitution of one emotional outlet for another is your favourite ploy.'

The Professor smiled. 'You Shetlanders are essentially individualists, a race of people who, probably because of your islands' comparative isolation, accept as your right a freedom many mainlanders envy, the freedom of being master of your own destiny, of being allowed to make your own decisions and to keep your own counsel. Always you prefer to toil alone against whatever adverse conditions you may encounter—consequently, in order to prise out the truth, I was forced to break down the barrier of undemonstrative equanimity that is so ingrained in your character. Unfortunately, the most effective method I know of making a woman angry is to cast doubt upon her morals—am I forgiven . . .?'

Her deepening blush implied that he was not, nevertheless, to his relief, she responded with a brief nod.

'Good. Then now that we have disposed of ambiguities, let us examine all the relevant facts. As I understand it, Catriona, you feel duty bound to abandon your career in order to look after an aged aunt who shouldered the responsibilities of both your parents when you were orphaned as a child?'

'As an infant,' she reminded him, 'a baby less than one year old. But duty plays no part——'

'Oh, but it does, my dear,' the Professor interrupted smoothly. 'Because, at a time of desperate need, your aunt—who must have been well past middle age at the time and a spinster to boot—stepped into the breach and dedicated the rest of her life to your upbringing, you feel morally obliged to abandon your own plans and ambitions now that the position has been reversed and she has need of you.'

'I suppose you're right,' she admitted soberly.

'The time has come when the debt I owe to my aunt must be repaid.'

'Hmm . . .' The Professor pressed the tips of his fingers together and studied them thoughtfully. 'But have you ever considered the possibility that your aunt might not view the situation in exactly the same light as yourself? Isn't it just possible,' he bent forward to urge, 'that your aunt, living in an isolated croft on a sparsely populated island and without any living creatures other than farm animals to call her own, might actually have welcomed the prospect of bringing a child into her home? Every human being, however self-sufficient, however much inclined to be unsociable, needs love, my dear. Knowing the depth of affection you feel for the old lady I have no doubt that, if asked, she would protest that the debt you feel is owing was repaid long ago.'

Catriona stared then, casting him a look of amazement, rose slowly to her feet. 'Are you actually suggesting that I should seize upon that theory as a salve to my conscience, an excuse to abandon my aunt in her hour of need?' The Professor jerked upright in his seat when, activated by anger, the girl known throughout the university for her calm self-possession, for a detachment so complete flirtatious male colleagues had been known to mutter accusations of frigidity, became suddenly alive—a transformation swift as the whipping of an expressionless mask from the face of a flushed, angry woman. 'You can have little concept of life as it's lived in my part of the world, Professor, or you wouldn't put forward the theory that a show of affection might be sufficient repayment for the years of backbreaking work, the

scrimping and saving, the worry and doubt, that my
aunt endured in order to ensure that I was kept
clothed and fed and, most important of all in her
eyes, that I had books, books and more books to
study. We existed by being self-sufficient, living in a
house that's no more than a stone built "but and
ben" with a whitewashed hearth and an open fire
fuelled with peat that my aunt cut and stacked herself. She also grew corn and hay, enough each year
to fill the barn attached to the house; knitted jumpers
from wool rooed from our own sheep, and cultivated
vegetables in the kale yard, a piece of land sheltered
from wind and weather by a stone dyke. I never
went hungry—indeed, since leaving Shetland I don't
believe I've tasted anything to compare with my
aunt's home-grown potatoes; tender, heather-fed
mutton and lamb; or the delicacy we enjoyed as a
special treat, piltock fish caught by ourselves during
long summer evenings, sufficient, when salted and
dried, to keep us supplied all through the winter
months. I was blessed with a happy childhood and a
full and satisfying adolescence, Professor,' she declared
so fiercely he was startled by the reminder that in the
veins of all Shetlanders was mingled the blood of old
Norse raiders; that she could probably claim kinship
with a race that had bred the Valkyries—twelve
maidens of Valhalla who, mounted on swift horses
and holding drawn swords, had rushed into the mêlée
of battle and selected those destined to die.

'. . . so please, never again suggest that a kiss on
the cheek or even a sackful of money might be valid
recompense for years of selfless devotion!'

'Phew!' The Professor looked shocked and for the

first time in his life completely nonplussed, astounded by the realisation that the girl he had labelled a quiet, studious dreamer was in reality an enigma, a character as paradoxical as lava seething molten beneath a crust of frozen snow. 'Calm down, my dear,' he pleaded when eventually he found his voice, I'm sorry if I've angered you—believe me, this time it was not intentional.'

For a second it seemed that his apology had not registered, then much to his relief Catriona's furious sparkle drained as quickly as the tempestuous colour from her cheeks. Looking slightly dazed, she stepped backward, then when her hand touched wood she sank down into her chair.

'I'm sorry,' she gasped, 'I don't know what came over me. I know you're only trying to help, but believe me, there's nothing you can do. After exploring every avenue of hope I've been forced to conclude that I have no choice but to return home.'

'Yes, it would appear so, my dear.' Reluctantly he conceded the necessity of being deprived of the services of his valued assistant. 'But how will your aunt react to the news, do you suppose? Knowing how fiercely independent she is, how proud of your success, I suspect she may object.'

'I'm certain she will,' Catriona laughed shakily. 'Thinking up a convincing excuse for returning home has been my biggest headache. To pretend to have been fired would cause an almighty row; to use redundancy as an excuse would only result in her insisting on my searching for a position farther afield, for there are no employment opportunities in

Shetland other than those connected with the oil companies.'

The Professor looked puzzled. 'Any firm would count itself fortunate to be given the opportunity of employing the services of such a highly qualified secretary as yourself, my dear, yet you appear to consider a job with the oil company an unlikely prospect?'

She shifted uncomfortably, embarrassed by the need to confess to having been secretly seeking alternative employment. 'I've already been turned down by the oil company in question,' she admitted stiffly, struggling to control a blush of half-mortified, half-guilty colour. 'Just a couple of weeks ago, Lion Oil Incorporated advertised a staff vacancy at its onshore terminal, based conveniently near to my home in Shetland. Applicants were invited to apply for the position of private secretary to their Director of Operations, and as the list of required qualifications seemed well within my range of capabilities I applied immediately, hardly able to believe the lucky coincidence that had made such a rare and suitable post available at precisely the right moment. Unfortunately,' her sigh echoed with puzzled regret, 'I received a reply almost by return of post informing me in brief, bald sentences that my letter had been received but that, regrettably, my name couldn't be included in the short list of suitable applicants.'

'Just that?' the Professor queried indignantly, 'No explanation as to why a highly skilled secretary, possessing the added advantage of having been raised on the island, should have her application turned down without even being granted the courtesy of an interview?'

'I'm afraid so,' Catriona shrugged, attempting to make light of deep disappointment, 'but no doubt they have a valid reason, after all, world-wide recession is forcing firms to make more and more valued employees redundant, consequently, the number of proficient secretaries willing to accept work in isolated, inhospitable regions must have risen considerably.'

'Exactly,' the Professor nodded, 'which is why I find the oil company's decision to pass over your application for employment so extraordinary. I have just recalled to mind a conversation I had with the chairman of one of the companies at present drilling for oil in the Shetland basin. The occasion was a symposium organised by the oil companies in order to outline the developments planned for that area over the next two decades. It was while we were discussing the dangers faced by men working in such dangerous waters that the subject of the difficulties arising from a colossal industrial development plonked into the midst of a small, tightly knit community was raised. Apparently, following protracted, noisy, and often acrimonious arguments with the local authorities the Shetland Islands Council was formed to protect the interests of the islanders, a surprisingly formidable body made up of local residents which the oil executives grudgingly admitted turned out to be more than a match for their own experienced negotiators. Displaying the bargaining acumen of Arabs trading in the marketplace, as one oil man put it with reluctant admiration, the Council persuaded the oil company to agree to allow them power of control over all sea areas within three miles of the terminal; to act as harbour authority; purchase land for oil-related development, and also they extracted a promise from the oil men to compensate the islanders by paying a large amount of money into a 'disturbance fund' and to co-operate in every way possible in order to ensure that the residents of Shetland gained maximum benefit from an industrial development so high-powered it tends to dominate everything within its vicinity. Preferential treatment to be given to islanders seeking employment was one of the perks I heard mentioned as a sop to appease the resentment of locals who view the appearance of the oil men as a threat to the islands' traditional way of life.' His frowning glance swung towards her. 'I assume, Catriona, that you made it plain in your letter of application that you are a resident of Shetland?'

'Yes . . . certainly I did,' she stammered, confused by the Professor's train of thought, 'I also explained why I was finding it necessary to leave my university post and why it's imperative that I find work within travelling distance of the home I shall be sharing with an elderly, ailing aunt.'

'And still they didn't relent!' Goaded into action, the Professor rose to his feet and strode around his desk towards her. Cupping a hand beneath her elbow, he urged her out of the chair. 'Run along and keep yourself occupied for half an hour or so while I make a telephone call.' Barely allowing her feet time to touch the ground, he ushered her out of his study. 'But stay within call, for if my efforts should prove fruitful I may have to call upon you to reach an immediate decision.'

As her work was up to date and the Professor had not had time to dictate replies to his morning mail, she wandered deep in thought in the direction of the staff restroom, then veered at the last moment, deciding that she would have more opportunity to think in the more impersonal atmosphere of the university canteen. She had just settled down at a quiet corner table and begun stirring sugar into her coffee when a voice intruded into her absorption.

'If you stir much longer the spoon might dissolve, never mind the sugar!'

'Janelle!' Catriona welcomed her appearance with one of the rare, sweet smiles she reserved exclusively for special friends. 'How nice of you to join me for your coffee break.'

'I told you I would before we left the flat this morning, don't you remember? Really, Catriona,' Janelle grimaced, settling into the chair opposite, 'you've always been a dreamer, but since your return from holiday last week you seem to have been walking about in a daze! What's wrong, is something troubling you?'

Catriona bit her lip. She and Janelle, who was in charge of the university switchboard, had shared a flat for the past couple of years and had discovered that the arrangement suited them so well they had recently invested some of their joint savings in a Mini. The change of circumstances was bound to hit Janelle hard, therefore she was entitled to be told the worst so that she could be given as much time as possible to find another flatmate willing to share expenses.

'I have some bad news, I'm afraid,' she plunged

without preamble. 'I must return home soon—
permanently.'

'What? Leave university . . .!' Janelle's wiry
copper hair seemed almost to stand on end. 'But you
love it here—you live, sleep and eat work, you have
no other interest in life!'

Wincing from this blunt home truth, Catriona
began outlining the reason behind her decision in a
few concise sentences, and when she had finished her
friend looked stunned, her expression a mixture of
dismay, pity and shock. It said much for the regard
they shared when, instead of dwelling upon her own
personal difficulties, Janelle's first consideration was
Catriona's welfare.

'But what will you find to *do*?' she almost wailed.
'I gather from what you've told me that Shetland
comprises a cluster of remote islands, mostly un-
inhabited, situated halfway between Norway and
Scotland and kept isolated from civilisation by the
cold North Sea!'

'There are mod cons available to those who can
afford them,' Catriona corrected with a smile, 'water
supply, electricity, television reception and so on. But
in my opinion, one of the most valuable assets the
islands possess is their air of tranquillity, a sense that
there's always time to spare and peace in which to
think and sort out the true order of priorities.'

'Peace shouldn't be difficult to find where there
are few marriageable men,' her forthright friend
retorted.

'I'm not interested in men, nor they in me,'
Catriona responded, unmoved.

'True, but they very soon would be if you'd stop

giving them the fast freeze treatment. If only you'd let your hair down—*literally* let your hair down, I mean,' Janelle giggled, 'although metaphorically speaking it wouldn't be such a bad idea either! That flaxen halo of yours is very becoming, but unfortunately it's apt to put men off. Whenever you glide into a room, dignified, aloof, and with a golden coronet shimmering around your head most men, especially the immature students who attend university functions, seem to suffer a severe bout of inferiority complex. Yet basically,' she sighed, 'you're a very feminine lady who ought never to go short of an escort. I'm no psychologist,' she nodded sagely, 'but I like people and take an interest in them, which is why I'm daring to stick out my neck and offer you some advice—if ever you feel like shouting then shout; if you want to scream then scream, and if ever a feller should take your fancy for heaven's sake let him know it!'

She peeped warily across her coffee cup, expecting a withering glance, but the sight of her friend's abstracted expression gave rise to a suspicion that she had been wasting her breath.

'Catriona!'

'What . . .? Oh, I do beg your pardon,' Catriona jerked. 'I'm sorry, I'm afraid my thoughts were far away. Would you mind repeating your question?'

But even while Janelle was expelling an exasperated sigh a message was relayed over the tannoy.

'*Attention, please! Will Miss Catriona Dunross contact Professor Sandwick's office immediately—repeat immediately!*'

The moment she stepped inside the Professor's

study Catriona was struck by his expression of great satisfaction.

'Sit down, my dear.' He waved her towards a chair. 'I have good news. I believe I've managed to achieve a solution to your problem!'

'You have . . .?' In spite of his obvious high spirits she sounded doubtful, unconvinced.

'Almost certainly,' he beamed, looking perversely pleased, considering the objections he had raised immediately he had read her letter of resignation earlier that morning, 'I've just finished speaking on the telephone to my old friend, Sir Donald Brierly, Chairman of Lion Oil Incorporated. I managed to reach him at his London office and promptly demanded an enquiry into why my personal assist-ant, a secretary proficient in every aspect of office procedure, utterly trustworthy, completely reliable, and with references second to none, should have had her application for employment with his company so arbitrarily and unfairly dismissed. Naturally, I had to outline your domestic circumstances, my dear,' he looked only slightly apologetic, 'otherwise he would have begun wondering why I seemed anxious to be rid of such a paragon, but once the position had been explained he was most co-operative. As I know to my cost, maintaining cordial relations between his oil men and local residents is an obsession with him, so much so that he's apt to become boring whenever he launches upon the subject. Consequently, it was not difficult to guide the con-versation in our—or rather, your—favour, the upshot being that Sir Donald declared himself well satisfied with my personal recommendation and, dismissing the need for any enquiry or even for consultation with his Shetland-based personnel, has stated firmly and categorically that, if you should still be interested, the position of secretary to the Director of Operations is yours!'

Catriona blinked, undecided whether to stamp her foot with vexation or throw her arms around the out-of-touch, slightly pompous Professor whose elevated status kept him immune from petty jealousies seething beneath the surface of office equanimity that needed only a hint of patronage, a whiff of favouritism, to rear its ugly head.

'Well, Catriona, what do you say, are you willing to accept the position?'

In spite of lurking misgivings, a mind swirling with trepidation and doubt, she knew that she could not afford to allow such a timely opportunity to slip out of her grasp.

'More than willing, Professor,' she gulped. 'Eager, grateful, hardly able to believe my luck!'

'Good.' He allowed himself the luxury of a self-congratulatory grin. 'Then I suggest that you begin preparing to leave at the end of the week. When you arrive at the terminal in Shetland you're to report to the Director of Operations, a gentleman by the name of Leon Casson.'

She was wandering, bemused, towards the door when he halted her in her tracks.

'Oh, by the way, Sir Donald hinted that this man Casson might turn out to be a little . . . er . . . uncooperative. If he should give you any trouble, Catriona, stand your ground, insist upon being granted all the rights laid down in your contract of employment—and don't hesitate to remind him that your appointment has been personally approved by the Chairman of the Board!'

CHAPTER TWO

IT was a rare, bright day with, for once, no shroud of mist hanging around the islands. Brilliant sunshine had turned the choppy North Sea a lighter shade of grey, and as Catriona stared out of the window the silhouette of the helicopter reflected upon the water reminded her of a grotesque sea monster forging steadily beneath the waves.

'We're almost ready to land, Miss Dunross, I hope you had an enjoyable flight?'

Catriona looked up to see a young, smartly-uniformed stewardess smiling down at her.

'Surprisingly enjoyable, thank you. I arrived at the heliport prepared to endure a bumpy, noisy ride sitting next to the pilot inside a miniature craft far removed from this luxurious forty-four-seater. Certainly I didn't anticipate enjoying the attention of two very pleasant stewardesses.'

The girl looked pleased. 'The men who work on our oil patch deserve the very best, Miss Dunross, the work they undertake is fast, tough and extremely demanding. Come to think of it,' she smiled, 'that's also a fair description of their attitude towards re-creation! As you're entitled to use company transport you must obviously be a new recruit to our on-shore base,' she continued, displaying friendly curiosity. 'Starting out on a new job is a difficult time and you must be anxious to create a good impression.

Naturally, my job brings me into contact with all oil company personnel, so if you'd care to tell me the name of your immediate superior I might be able to help by putting you wise to any personal quirks or idiocyncrasies.'

Catriona hesitated. The girl had shrewdly concluded that she was about to join the staff of oil field secretaries, and though she had no wish to discuss the nature of her work neither did she want to snub the girl's friendly overture. Opting for diplomacy, she murmured,

'I've been employed to take over the post of private secretary to Leon Casson, the Director of Operations.'

'You're going to work with Leo the Lion?'

Catriona's spirits zoomed to zero when the girl dropped into the adjacent seat projecting an attitude that was a mixture of shock, pity and downright awe. But at the sight of her frown the stewardess attempted a quick recovery.

'Don't let the designation put you off. The title, coined by some of his more irreverent employees, probably alludes more to the fact that he's in charge of Oilfield Lion than to any personal characteristics. The boss pilots his own helicopter, but on the few occasions he has flown with us I've found him extremely charming,' she blushed, somehow managing to convey to Catriona an image of a tawny-eyed, predatory male preening with chauvinist conceit.

She dismissed the thought from her mind and cleared her throat, annoyed with herself for feeling nervous.

'I've been told that there are a great number of

overseas personnel employed by the oil company?'
She paused delicately, calculating that her query
would immediately become associated in the girl's
mind with the subject of their current conversation.

'Leon Casson came originally from the States—
Texas, I believe—but according to girls working at
base he's travelled the world for so many years,
working on oilfields as far distant as the Persian Gulf,
Mexico and even Alaska, he's lost all allegiance to
any one country and is considered to be more a citi-
zen of the world,' the starry-eyed stewardess did not
disappoint her.

'Would I be right in assuming that he's remained
a bachelor?' Catriona probed, anxious to collate as
much background information as possible before
meeting the man who she instinctively sensed was
about to present problems.

'You are indeed,' the girl laughed aloud. 'In
spite of the many girls who've fancied their chance
as a lion-tamer he has guarded his liberty well
and continues roaming free, creating havoc among
the females inhabiting his particular patch of
jungle.'

Catriona had to admire the efficiency of a company which, when she alighted from the helicopter,
proved itself to be equally well informed about the
arrival of its newest recruit as it was about VIPs. A
car was waiting to drive her the short distance between the heliport and a huge complex of accommo-
dation and administration buildings; storage tanks;
processing plant; docks, garages, workshops and
dozens of unidentifiable buildings that formed the
pulse of Lion Oil Incorporated, the on-shore base

from which determined treasure-seekers directed the search for fluid gold.

'I have the number of the chalet you've been allocated in the village, miss,' the laconic, gum-chewing driver tossed across his shoulder, 'but the boss seems eager to make your acquaintance. Usually, new recruits are given time to unpack their bags before being summoned into his presence, but my instructions are to drive you straight from the airport to his office, so, rather than risk having my guts used for garters, that's exactly what I aim to do!'

'I shan't be living in the village,' she corrected, 'my home is less than half an hour's drive from here, so I intend commuting daily.'

'Oh, so you're a local?' His eyebrows, reflected in the driving mirror, elevated with surprise. 'In that case there's no fear of you being lonely—a large percentage of our work force is made up of local inhabitants. Also many of the staff who came here when the terminal first opened have had houses built and brought their families over to settle in Shetland permanently. Personally, I'm content to live in the village, the chalets are clean and comfortable, the food is first class, and there are sufficient bars, concert rooms, restaurants and recreation halls to cater for all tastes. The entertainment is especially good. Do you like jazz, miss?' Without waiting to hear her reply, he continued on a note of great anticipation. 'One of the country's top jazz bands has been booked to play in the concert hall this weekend. Even if you don't live on the site, as one of the work force you're entitled to attend.'

'Thank you for letting me know,' Catriona responded, made slightly breathless by the discovery

that the barren acreage of land shunned as expend-
able even by tenacious, hard-working islanders had
been transformed by superbly efficient, high-
powered organisation into a bustling hive of activity.
'As yet, I'm uncertain about my plans for the weekend, but if it's at all possible I'd like to go to the
concert. Where can I get a ticket?'

The driver's chewing jaws dropped open with surprise. Then he began to chuckle. 'Bless you, miss,
you won't find tickets on sale here, all entertainment
is free—and no seats can be reserved, not even for
management. All you need do when you arrive at
the concert hall is pile inside with the rest of the
crowd and claim the first available seat!'

Their arrival outside of the main office building
put an end to the conversation. Hesitating on the
threshold of the surprisingly smart, modern building
just long enough to smooth the creases from her skirt,
Catriona drew in a deep, steadying breath and
marched inside.

'Good morning, can I help you?'

A young, chic, incredibly voluptuous receptionist
looked up as she approached the desk.

'If you'd be so kind,' Catriona gulped, made uncomfortably aware that to fashion-conscious eyes her
neat, willow green jumper suit might appear slightly
dated. 'I was instructed to report immediately I
arrived to the Director of Operations.'

'The boss is carrying out a tour of the base at the
moment, Miss . . .?'

'Dunross—Catriona Dunross. I'm to be the
Director's new secretary.'

The girl's pencil-stroked eyebrows shot skyward.

'Then if you wouldn't mind waiting in his office, Miss Dunross, the boss won't keep you long, he's due to arrive back any minute now.'

She walked from behind the reception area and began leading the way towards a row of teak-grained doors each bearing a nameplate. As Catriona followed obediently in her wake, her sensible brogues making soundless contact with a width of mirror-polished floor, her sense of inferiority was not improved by the sight of shapely legs encased in sheer black nylon and ankles beautified by the slenderising effect of strappy sandals perched upon high, finely tapering heels. 'Can I get you a cup of coffee?' the film star look-alike enquired, waiting until Catriona had settled into a leather armchair positioned strategically in front of a huge desk strewn with correspondence, discarded envelopes, manuals, maps, and a spread-out blueprint that appeared to show the layout of the base camp and adjoining oil terminal.

'No, thank you, I had some on the flight over,' she refused, striving to appear composed, her nervousness increasing as the ordeal loomed nearer. Immediately the door had closed behind the young receptionist she began fumbling inside her handbag for the owl-rimmed, amber-tinted spectacles purchased as a ploy to add a touch of maturity to youthful features, a shield of authority behind which she had hidden naïvety and basic shyness from some of the more worldly university students. She was adjusting the frames above the bridge of her nose when the door was flung open with force, causing a hurricane draught that rustled the papers on top of the desk and lifted the flimsy blueprint so that it floated, then began drifting downwards to the carpet. Instinctively, Catriona darted sideways to save it and collided with a violent bump against a solid obstacle that had appeared without warning, leaving her no time to check her propulsion. The moment her head connected with an iron-muscled chest, the moment her ears caught the sound of a breathed curse and her shoulders were captured in a bruising grip, she sensed that she had managed to upset the equilibrium of the oil king with the notoriously inflammable temper.

'Who the devil are you?'

Shock waves trembled through her limbs when, after being set down upon her heels with a thump that jarred every bone in her body, she came face to face not with the expensively suited, cigar-smoking executive she had expected but with a lean, rugged action-man type, all angles, sporting a checked workshirt, neckerchief, denims with decorative stitching almost obscured by faded oil stains, and a yellow protective helmet emblazoned with an emblem of a lion rampant centred directly above a line of dark frowning eyebrows. She backed away, blanching from vibes of sheer animal virility exuding from the man who appeared capable of disposing of any unwelcome recruit as easily as he would demolish a plate-size breakfast steak.

'I'm Catriona Dunross . . .' she stammered in total confusion, then, scrabbling for the cloak of cool possession that formed the major part of her armoury, she tilted her chin and continued with dignity. 'If you're Leon Casson, Director of Operations, then I'm your new secretary.'

'The devil you are!'

Dismissing her claim with infuriating contempt, he wheeled behind the desk to coil long fluid limbs into a chair.

'You don't look old enough to have left junior school, much less attained the giddy status of private secretary.'

'I can't help my looks,' she retorted, stiff with resentment.

'That's a debatable point,' he glittered, waving her back to her seat. In spite of herself she shivered when, with a smile playing around his lips and one booted foot hooked across a knee, he swivelled sideways in his chair to examine her thoroughly. Prickles of embarrassment chased up and down her spine as gold-flecked eyes stripped her piece by piece until she felt naked. Sweat damped her palms as she willed her expression to remain calm, fought hard to deprive him of the satisfaction of guessing that a childhood and schooldays spent entirely in the company of her own sex, and consequent years devoted entirely to academic study, had rendered her a stranger to male aggression, defenceless against the brutal audacity of a man who, either from choice or because of the haunts he had frequented, appeared to have become accustomed to viewing females as brainless dolls eager to flaunt their attractions, who invited male attention with looks that were bold, even brazen. 'It appears to me,' he annoyed her by drawling when finally he had concluded his assessment, 'that you could put much more effort into capitalising on your assets. But at least,' he grinned, 'you haven't cultivated a moustache which, had you been destined to remain here, I would certainly have found offensive.'

'What are you implying?' she croaked through a throat so dry she could barely force a whisper. 'I *am* remaining here. I've signed a contract of employment and I don't intend leaving whatever the circumstances!'

Not a muscle moved, not a flicker disturbed his impassive features. 'Had I been notified earlier of your imminent arrival you wouldn't have been allowed aboard the helicopter,' he shocked her by saying.

'But why?' In her agitation she whipped the amber shields from her eyes so that he received the full blast of her outraged glare. 'You need a secretary and I need a job—it's especially important that I find work here in Shetland where I can live at home and look after an elderly relative. I can meet all the requirements laid down in your advertisement—indeed, if anything I'm over-qualified for what appears to be a perfectly routine job, therefore what possible objection can you have, it can't be anything personal, since you don't even know me!'

'It was evident from your letter that you were female,' his response was so cool it took her breath away, 'and all applications from females were weeded out immediately. I employ male secretaries only, Miss Dunross, because experience has taught me that female secretaries—and especially immature infants such as yourself—are unable to cope with the pressures of the job.'

'But that's blatant sex discrimination!' she gasped.

'Obviously a man of your occupation is cut off from civilisation, yet I'd imagined that news of the Sex Discrimination Act, introduced some years ago, would by now have filtered even as far as the oil-fields!' She could have bitten off her tongue the moment the snide statement had been made, not because she regretted the dart she had directed towards his tough hide, but because she could not afford the luxury of jeopardising her chances of gaining the job she needed so desperately. It seemed incredible that Leon Casson could be unaware that he was breaking the law, yet deciding to give him the benefit of the doubt, she said more gently. 'It's now unlawful in this country, Mr Casson, for a female applicant to be treated less favourably than a man merely on the grounds of her sex.'

Immediately frowning eyebrows drew into a thick dark underscore beneath the rim of his steel helmet and amber eyes flashed sparks of temper through a thicket of lashes she sensed that he had mistaken her genuine attempt to enlighten for patronage.

'I'm almost tempted to punish your impudence by giving you the job as my secretary, Miss Dunross, but to do so a man would need to be so lacking in conscience he would feel no qualms about throwing a rabbit to a pack of wolves.' Coldly, tersely, he flayed her confidence, spitting words from his lips as he would have spat a mouthful of gravel. 'I'm completely *au fait* with the rules and regulations governing the employment of workers. In my capacity as Director of Operations I'm kept snowed under with piles of correspondence and miles of red tape directed by Government departments of this, that or the other—which is why I'm in urgent need of a replacement for the assistant whose initiative and competence have been rewarded with higher status. If you'd researched the subject more thoroughly you would have discovered that there are exceptions to the rules governing the Sex Discrimination Act, one of them being the disqualification of any applicant whose sex can be proved to be a genuine occupational hazard. Another, applying solely to females, states that legislation limits the times at which females may work, and also declares out of bounds certain types of location. As you will have judged for yourself from my present outfit, Miss Dunross, I'm far from office-bound. Touring the terminal, checking the docks, flying by 'copter out to the rig can be rough, tough, and very often dangerous, and wherever I go I prefer my secretary—or as I prefer to call him, my assistant—to accompany me. Do I need to go on?'

With a throat so painfully tight she found it impossible to speak she struggled to assimilate the knowledge that the solution of what to do about her aunt had been thoroughly scuttled. She stared, conscious of his triumph yet too dazed to actually register his expression, feeling cruelly cheated, wondering how on earth she was to explain her arrival at the cottage later that day, wondering how long, provided she did eventually manage to persuade her aunt to allow her to stay, the small amount of money she had saved would last without a salary to boost her bank account. The thought crossed her mind of appealing to Leon Casson's better nature, then was immediately dismissed as ludicrous. Even without the stewardess's verbal illustration of the company boss, or the receptionist's obvious eagerness to flaunt her attractions, she would have had no difficulty classifying Leon Casson as a blatant sexist, a man whose ego demanded the nourishment of being made to feel superior, macho, chauvinistically contemptuous of the physical strength and mental agility of what he would no doubt term the weaker sex. Nevertheless, for the sake of her aunt, she felt she could not give up without a fight.

'Physically, I'm very fit,' she insisted, jutting a determined chin, 'also, for four years I attended further education classes five nights a week while holding down a full-time job, which must prove that I'm capable of working long hours at a stretch.'

He smiled unpleasantly. 'Often, while visiting the rig, the weather deteriorates to such an extent that I'm forced to live in until conditions improve,' he squashed, his tone mellowed by complacency. 'As the rig is an all-male establishment, separate sleeping quarters for females are not available.'

'I don't see that as an insuperable problem,' Catriona persisted doggedly. 'You could imagine I'm just another man, in fact I'd prefer you to. A sleeping bag tucked away in some quiet corner would suit me fine!'

'No way,' he drawled, shaking his head while an infuriating smile played around his lips. 'Either you're a nymphomaniac, Miss Dunross, or you're entirely ignorant of the nature of the men who work on oil rigs—supermen, risk-takers extraordinary, hell-raisers who feel entitled to let off steam whenever they manage a break from working in freezing temperatures. Never would I allow men in superb physical condition, deprived for weeks upon end of female company, to have their minds distracted from their dangerous work by the sight of a shapely ankle or a sensuous, wiggling walk.'

The humiliation of being classed as a mindless sex object goaded her beyond reason. Fixing his mocking face with eyes glittering vixen bright, spitting darts of feline fury, she blazed,

'Must I remind you that the decision to employ my services was approved by no less a personage than your company Chairman?'

She shrivelled inwardly, yet stood her ground, determined not to betray a leap of terror-ridden pulses when he leant forward across the desk, his slit-narrow eyes, flaring nostrils and curling upper lip suddenly robbed of humour. By contrast, his low throaty growl was doubly shocking.

'Our Chairman, a fellow director and veteran diver like myself, is a man who's worked his way to the top, becoming deservedly admired and respected not only for his drive and ambition, but because he has proved over the years that he's always prepared to listen to constructive criticism and to reverse any decision that might eventually be proved wrong.'

'But he's also,' she argued recklessly, 'a man who places harmony between oil men and local residents very high on his list of priorities, so much so that he agreed wholeheartedly with our Council's suggestion that islanders should be given first preference when applying to fill job vacancies.' She waited, glowing with the satisfaction of a gambler who has suddenly discovered a hidden trump card, then when he made no haste to respond she stabbed deeper. 'No doubt you'll be able to persuade your Chairman around to your way of thinking, but it could take time. Indeed, the argument might turn out to be quite lengthy. Didn't I hear you mention that you're an extremely busy man, Mr Casson?' she enquired with deliberate sweetness. 'And also that you're very much hampered by the lack of a secretary?'

When their glances clashed Catriona experienced real fear for the first time in her life, fear of a thin smile that was like the baring of the fangs of a jungle king prepared to leap straight at the jugular vein; fear of the snap of white teeth and the angry expression on a face so tanned by exposure to wind and salt spray it resembled the dark, even brown of flesh cured over smouldering oak chips.

'You are obstinate, stubborn, and obviously out to make trouble, Miss Dunross,' he menaced across the width of his desk. 'However, such persistence should not go unrewarded.' With shocking suddenness he lunged to his feet and strode towards the door. 'I've changed my mind,' he snapped. 'Be prepared to start work in this office at eight-thirty sharp tomorrow morning!'

Before she could gasp her gratitude the door banged shut behind him, leaving her stunned, doubtful, her mind pounding with words culled from the memory of a Shakespeare play she had enjoyed months previously.

'Yond Cassius has a lean and hungry look:
He thinks too much: such men are dangerous.'

CHAPTER THREE

A WORRIED quirk played around Catriona's lips as she sat in the rear seat of the chauffeur-driven car summoned so swiftly that its appearance had provided fair indication of the oil boss's anxiety to be rid of her. Her victory had been won so incredibly easily, especially considering the fact that her meagre knowledge of how to handle men had been gleaned solely from conversations overheard at students' halls and in teachers' restrooms. *'Man has a hole in his mind plastered over with conceit!'* one particularly unscrupulous girl had stated. *'Never feel guilty about scoring off any man—he'll be carrying his comfort around with him.'*

Instinct told her that such an outlook was wrong, yet from the moment she had set foot inside Leon Casson's domain her personality had seemed to split into two separate entities—the calm, unemotional girl suddenly submerged by the passionate, unpredictable, completely irrational woman.

She sat tense, unable to enjoy the half-hour journey along a coast road with a landscape dominated by sea, surging, rolling, thrusting into long narrow voes, creaming around the bases of jagged cliffs, washing beaches stretching solitary and smooth along secretive, picturesque coves. Piles of ancient stone reared occasionally upon the treeless skyline, ruined forts testifying to the skill and ingenuity of civilisations that had inhabited the islands many centuries ago.

Catriona craned her neck and peered inland when she recognised a familiar stretch of bare, unrelieved moorland, eager for her first sight of a dot upon the horizon that would signal that she was almost home.

'Not far now,' she told the surprised driver. 'See that croft house just visible on the horizon—please drop me off there.'

'That old thatched cottage?' he peered hard. 'It looks deserted, I'd no idea people still lived in such places.'

'Live *and* work,' she smiled without taking offence. 'If you look farther to the left you'll see a figure cutting peat on the hillside.'

'Peat!' the modern-minded young man snorted. 'Give me central heating any time.'

Catriona shrugged. 'Obviously you've been denied the pleasure of sitting over a glowing peat fire in winter time, sniffing its pleasant, mildly antiseptic smell, basking in heat as intense as any given out by other solid fuels, yet lacking the soot and dirtiness of most of them.'

When the young driver drove off, after promising to return for her early the next morning, she began making her way up to the peat hill, keeping her eyes fastened upon the gaunt figure stooped over her task of laying out turves of peat in neat walls to dry. Her brow puckered as she noted the slow, laboured movements, the stiff, agonised straightening of the spine, the stumbling steps of her aunt who, not many months ago, had boasted with truth that she possessed the energy and agility of a fifty-year-old.

'Leave that!' she called out, anxiety making her tone sharper than she had intended. 'I'll finish it later.'

'Who's there?' To Catriona's utter dismay her aunt's eyes, trained directly upon her, seemed to be providing her with very limited vision. Conscious of the old lady's pride, her reluctance to admit to any degree of disability, she forbore any mention of failing eyesight and responded with forced lightness.

'It's me . . . Catriona. I didn't write to warn you of my arrival, I wanted to surprise you.'

'Catriona!' The tuskar her aunt had been using to cut peat fell from her grasp as she opened her arms wide to receive her. 'My bonny bairn, what a wonderful surprise, I was just thinking about you!'

Yet even though Catriona felt a suspicion of moisture on her aunt's cheeks while they exchanged hugs and kisses the basically undemonstrative old lady pushed her away to scold sternly. 'You've no right to give a body such a fright! Anyway, what's brought you here in the middle of term, is something the matter?'

'Why, whenever there's the slightest deviation from normal, must you jump to the conclusion that something is wrong?'

'Because I'm suspicious of change,' her aunt snapped, 'I like things to go on as they've always done.'

'I know you do, Aunt Hanna,' Catriona laughed aloud, 'but I can assure you that this is a happy visit. Let's go inside the house and I'll explain.'

Once inside the tiny living-room with firelight reflecting from shiny brasses; square-paned windows draped with flowered chintz to match covers on cushions and chairs; old, faded rugs placed strategically on spots where resting feet were most likely to need protection from the ever-present chill rising from a stone-flagged floor, Catriona prepared herself for an inquisition. She did not have long to wait. Immediately a black kettle singing on a hook suspended above the firegrate had boiled, then the teapot filled and set between them on the table while they waited for the brew to 'mash' the old lady demanded,

'Now, tell me exactly why you're in Shetland when you ought to be at university?'

Treading warily, made uneasy by the knowledge that never once in her lifetime had she been able to deceive her aunt and that, on the few reckless occasions when she had tried, retribution had been swift, she decided to stick as closely to the truth as possible.

'I applied for a post with the oil company and was fortunate enough to be accepted by the Director of Operations as his private secretary. I shall be working here on the island, Aunt Hanna,' she urged brightly, 'and as transport is provided for all employees resident on Shetland I shall be able to live at home permanently and commute to work each day.'

Hoping for a favourable response, she kept her fingers crossed beneath the table, yet was not completely unprepared when wise old eyes, bird-bright with suspicion, were trained upon her flushed face.

'I don't understand,' her aunt frowned severely. 'You've always seemed so happy with your job at the university—often you've said how much you enjoy working with Professor Sandwick and how you could never hope to repay him for his kindness and for the interest he's taken in your career. I've heard that the oil people pay exorbitant wages—as if they have to *bribe* people to work here—but you've never been a mercenary person, praise be, so money can be discounted as the motive behind your extraordinary decision. Tell me the truth, Catriona,' she demanded sharply, 'what's your real reason for turning your back upon a job you love, the friends you've made, and worst of all, upon Professor Sandwick, the man to whom you owe so much loyalty?'

Uncomfortable as a schoolgirl squirming beneath the eye of an angry headmistress, Catriona responded with an almost indistinct mumble.

'Loyalties often become divided, Aunt Hanna, tearing one apart as the mind dictates one course of action and the heart another.'

'The heart . . .?' Aunt Hanna snapped. 'What on earth have your emotions to do with a change of employment?' Then to Catriona's surprise she gave a loud gasp, then relaxed, a smile of pleasure spreading across her features.

'What a blind, stupid old woman I am,' she chuckled softly, 'and how shy you still must be, child, if you can't bring yourself to spell out in words of one syllable why you've allowed your heart to dictate your actions. You're in love,' she decided with great satisfaction, 'and obviously the object of your affection is employed by the local oil company! Did you imagine, Kate, my dear,' her bright eyes scolded, 'that just because I've remained a spinster I couldn't understand or excuse your desire to put less distance between yourself and the man you love?'

'The man I . . .!'

To anyone with clearer vision Catriona's astonished expression would have given the game away, but her aunt's weak eyesight was further dimmed by tears of sheer joy. Teetering on the brink of contradiction, Catriona hesitated, her conscience corrupted by a wicked inner voice whispering: '*Why not play along? It's such a heaven-sent excuse—and after all, there are times when a lie becomes permissible if one is certain that to tell the truth would be to invite anger, upset and endless recrimination.*'

'Now, child,' her aunt glowed, betraying a streak of romanticism Catriona had never suspected, 'tell me all about this remarkable young man who's managed to entice you away from your beloved university!'

Sensing that in order to satisfy her aunt's romantic expectations the description would have to be larger than life, a profile etched sharp as flint upon a background of slate, Catriona drew upon the image of the only man of her acquaintance who could even remotely match up to such requirements. Nervous as a diver about to explore uncharted seas, she plunged boldly into a depth of deception.

'He's a tough-talking, hard-bitten Texan, Aunt Hanna, a company executive and ex-diver who I suspect would much prefer to be back working with his team of North Sea treasure-hunters—men who can be compared with astronauts exploring outer space, inasmuch as they require the same qualities of courage, expertise and superb physical fitness in order to overcome underwater perils as great and as unexpected as any encountered by spacemen exploring the galaxy.'

'*Really?*' Her aunt expelled an admiring breath. 'How exciting!' She almost bounced out of her chair. 'And how wonderful to have fallen in love with a man of such high calibre—spirited, daring, intelligent, full of vitality—exactly the sort of qualities I'd hoped you'd find in the man you decided to marry.'

'Marry . . .?' Catriona sensed the situation getting out of hand. 'Who said anything about getting married?—you're presuming far too much, Aunt Hanna.'

'Not at all.' Her aunt's chin jutted. 'I'm well aware that some modern-minded misses are prepared to settle for less, but don't you be tempted, Catriona, play your fish by all means, tempt him with tasty bait, but keep him dangling on the hook until he's well and truly landed!'

'Aunt Hanna, I'm shocked!' Catriona gurgled, amazement giving way to amusement. 'I never imagined the day would dawn when I'd hear you advocating setting bait for humans!'

To her dismay, instead of responding in a jocular vein her aunt suddenly seemed to crumple, her happy twinkle fading until her eyes appeared glazed.

'Is it so wrong of me to want to see you married before I die, child?'

Catriona froze, alarmed by a sigh laden heavily with the acceptance of old age.

'I've never been lonely,' her aunt continued sadly.

'Solitude has always been my home and I've been content that it should be so, yet having said that, I must admit that when I was younger I felt occasional regret at having been denied the sense of fulfilment that only a husband and children can bring.' Abruptly, she jerked forward in her chair to emphasise, 'That is what I want for you, Kate dear . . .' Only during rare emotional moments did she revert to the diminutive she had often used to call Catriona in from play; to greet her arrival home from school. '. . . I feel weary, ready to relinquish my bonds, but not until I've seen you settled can I ever contemplate preparing to meet my Maker.'

With a cry of distress Catriona slid to her knees by the old lady's chair. 'Aunt Hanna, you're not to talk like that, I won't listen to you!' she choked, appalled by the realisation that her aunt's fierce pride in her ability to work, to converse intelligently, to read without the aid of spectacles or to labour lovingly over the fine lace shawls that grew beneath her nimble fingers from a few single stitches into an intricate web—large enough to spread across her lap, fine enough to be drawn through a wedding ring— had faded with her agility, leaving her prey to the temptation to live in the past, to dismiss all personal plans for the future. Every vestige of the guilt she had felt was dispersed from her conscience as, fiercely glad that she had lied, she seized upon the deception as a form of shock therapy.

Forcing herself to rise casually to her feet, she swept a critical eye around the tiny living-room. 'I hadn't noticed until this minute,' she censured, 'how shabby the house has become. A coat of distemper wouldn't come amiss and a lick of paint would make a vast improvement.'

As she had hoped, her remarks raised the old lady's interest as well as her blood pressure.

Daring to push her luck, she continued, tongue-in-cheek. 'As you seem eager to meet my friend no doubt you'll soon be inviting him to dinner, but before you do, oughtn't we to try to get the house looking a little more respectable?'

'*Respectable!*' Her aunt bridled to her feet seething with injured pride. 'Since when has my house not been considered respectable enough for visitors? I'll have you know, my girl, that these walls are distempered at least twice a year, and as for the paintwork, it was last done . . . er . . .'

'Yes, aunt?' she prompted, outwardly severe, but inwardly rejoicing. Knowing that her aunt, in common with most Shetlanders, possessed a deep vein of honesty, she was not surprised to see her colour rise before she admitted lamely,

'Well, perhaps I *have* been a little remiss in that respect.'

'In that case,' Catriona decided, carefully hiding her satisfaction, 'I'll telephone Lerwick tomorrow and ask the paint shop to deliver all the items we're likely to need.'

After a satisfying meal of vegetable broth followed by Finnan haddock—salted fish made easily recognisable by two 'fingerprints of Saint Peter' either side of its head, split, cleaned and salted, then slowly cured over smoking oak chips to a silver, tawny colour—they spent an hour deciding upon a new colour scheme, then retired early to bed, one to drift into sleep the moment her grey head touched the pillow, the other to lie awake for hours staring at the ceiling, wondering how best to cope, determined now more than ever to resort to any tactics, however questionable, in order to thwart the intention of the powerful oil boss who, in spite of his sudden capitulation, she suspected was still determined to be rid of her.

Mist was hanging low as her spirits, obliterating all familiar landmarks, when the chauffeur arrived an hour late at the cottage the following morning.

'If I'd known how rapidly visibility would diminish I wouldn't have set out at all,' he replied to Catriona's anxious enquiry about the time as they set off on the return journey. 'I know you've been told to report to the bosses office at eight-thirty, but I'm afraid you'll have to resign yourself to being at least a couple of hours late.'

'Why not let me drive?' she offered hastily. 'I've travelled this road so often on foot and by bicycle I'd know the way blindfolded.'

The driver's brow cleared. 'Well, if you're certain you don't mind, miss. Passengers are usually forbidden to take over the driving of company vehicles, but as I'm a stranger to this part of the island and have no wish to land the car in a ditch, and injure us both, I'll chance being carpeted by the boss for breaking the rules. He's a stickler for discipline, as you've probably gathered, he lays down the rules and has made it perfectly plain that no second chance will be given to anyone who doesn't abide by them.'

'Don't worry,' she reassured him, sliding confidently behind the wheel, 'not even a despot could argue with the logic of allowing a driver to take over whose knowledge of the district is superior. I know every bend and curve of this road,' she insisted, peering through mist rolling like waves against the windscreen. 'Even in this pea-souper, I know I can find my way back to the base with the minimum of delay.'

'Then I'll do my best to act as radar equipment, miss,' the driver grinned, settling sheepishly into the passenger seat. 'I'll keep my eyes peeled and let you know immediately the car seems in danger of running off the road.'

Pleased to discover him amenable to reason, Catriona started up the engine and began inching the car forward, increasing speed whenever the mist lifted long enough to disclose a clear stretch of road ahead.

'This must be the only length of road the oil company hasn't yet got around to improving,' her passenger grumbled when the offside tyres rumbled into a rut, jerking them both sideways. 'You Shelties must have found it hard to believe your good fortune when Lion Oil Incorporated moved into the island, providing better roads, houses, schools and medical facilities, improving air and sea communications and, most important of all, making available jobs with sky-high wages that have enabled families to buy luxuries previously far beyond their reach. I've heard there's been a phenomenal increase in the number of freezers, caravans, television sets and washing machines being delivered to the island.'

'As well as miles of ugly pipelines, sludge green

tanks, tons of cement and steel, and enough unsightly cable to stretch across to Europe and back,' she responded tartly, betraying her resentment of the despoiling of solitary heather-clad hills that had been gouged and flattened to make way for the sprawling oil terminal known to the locals as 'the light in the sky' because of the two million pounds' worth of flood lighting installed to enable men to work twelve hours a day right throughout the long Shetland winter when only six hours of murky daylight separated sunrise from sunset.

Perhaps it was the fact that he had been forced to hand over the wheel to a girl which was beginning to rankle, or maybe it was the depressing effect of thick grey mist, made all the more eerie by the mournful hoot of foghorns sounding a warning to tankers anchored offshore awaiting safe entry into the harbour, that made his response sound sour, hinting at her ingratitude.

'You natives are very hard to please! Even school-leavers can earn a couple of hundred pounds a week merely by sweeping out chalets and wiping down tables in bright modern surroundings designed to make workers feel less like prisoners condemned to a stretch of solitary confinement, yet your attitude towards oilmen remains frigid, none of you make any secret of the fact that you would prefer us to clear off your island—even though full advantage has been taken of company jobs and money.'

Irritated by his attitude, and by a slow rate of progress which she suspected was about to provide her impatient boss with an opportunity to exercise his sarcastic tongue on the subject of personnel who courted unpunctuality and caused inconvenience by insisting upon living off-site, Catriona defended smartly,

'Contrary to your opinion that oil has been our salvation, we were doing very nicely, thank you, before the arrival of treasure-hunters in search of black gold—perhaps not wealthy by oil mens' standards, but our knitwear and fishing industries were thriving, and our shops were stocked with everything necessary to supply our needs. Unfortunately, because of high wages dangled like carrots beneath the noses of youngsters, they began scorning local industries in favour of working for the oil company, but once the terminal is fully operational many workers will be made redundant and unemployment, which has never been a problem in Shetland, will become rife because knitting machines have been allowed to rust and fishing boats laid up through lack of labour!'

In the heat of the moment she took her eyes from the road just long enough to cast the driver a withering look and though her lapse of concentration was minimal, the time taken was sufficient to allow damage to be done. The moment her eyes slewed back towards the windscreen a dark patch of shadow loomed.

'Look out!' the driver yelled.

She braked, throwing him violently sideways, then swung the wheel hard around in an attempt to avoid hitting the shape that stood frozen for a second in the blaze of fog-lamps before bolting for cover under a blanket of thick mist. Frantically she spun the wheel in a reverse turn, but in spite of the car's crawling speed the correction came too late to prevent a sickening lurch when one side of the car tipped sideways into a ditch, leaving the remaining two wheels spinning madly about a foot above the surface of the road.

'Are you all right, miss?' In spite of their comparatively gentle landing the driver looked shocked, his face a white mask of concern peering out of the gloom.

'I . . . I think so.' She released her safety belt and gingerly stretched her limbs. 'Yes, I'm still in one piece—what about you?'

'Scared out of my wits! What the devil was that . . . *that thing* that loomed out of the mist?'

'Nothing more sinister than a Shetland pony,' she confessed ruefully. 'I'm sorry, I ought to have remembered that all during summer they're allowed the freedom of hills and moors and at times can become a bit of a nuisance. However, regrets will get us nowhere, the most pressing problem is how are we going to cover the last few miles between here and the base—walk?'

'Fortunately, that won't be necessary.' Leaning sideways out of the precariously tilted passenger seat, the driver reached beneath the dashboard towards what appeared to be a small black box that had protruding flex with a microphone attached. Keeping one hand upon the dashboard to maintain his balance, he fiddled with the controls to disperse noisy static before speaking into the microphone.

'Hello! Wheeler calling base. Wheeler calling base! I want to report an accident. Over!'

In a matter of seconds a female voice responded over the airways.

'Base to Wheeler. Come in, Wheeler, we're receiving you!'

Catriona slumped into her seat, then shot upright when a savage, clipped, masculine tone of authority crackled out of the receiver,

'Casson to Wheeler—what the blazes have you been up to, is anyone injured? State your position, then stay put until a breakdown gang arrives. Don't move a muscle or they'll never damn well find you!'

CHAPTER FOUR

SANDRA, the young receptionist whose sex signals seemed permanently set at green for 'come on', gave Catriona a surprisingly sympathetic look when at almost eleven o'clock, more than two hours after the time she should have begun work, she stumbled into reception and stood for a second to adjust her crumpled skirt, pat her hair into place, and erase all other signs of flustered haste.

Drawing upon experience gained while assisting Professor Sandwick in an experiment to test people's capacity to transmit moods and emotions without the use of words, Catriona, after studying her wardrobe carefully, had finally decided to wear a smart black dress buttoned high up to the neck, with long, tightly-cuffed sleeves and a slim-cut skirt tapering down to a hem settling a couple of respectable inches below the knee, hoping to transmit to her new boss a message of aloof reserve. But Sandra, whose loose open-weave sweater had been designed to provoke tantalising speculation as to whether or not its wearer was bra-less, obviously nurtured no such inhibitions.

'Prepare to be verbally mauled!' she hissed through glossy, plum coloured lips. 'The lion is rampant!'

'Thanks for the warning,' Catriona grimaced. 'I suppose he arrived at the office at eight-thirty prompt?'

'Goodness, no!' With a shake of her immaculately groomed head Sandra sent Catriona's spirits soaring before zooming them back to zero. 'Leon is a human powerhouse, he never starts work later than seven each morning. By the time you were due to arrive he had a pile of correspondence ready for your attention and between then and now he's had a meeting with union leaders, shared a working breakfast with middle management personnel, and he's now prowling his lair waiting for you to accompany him to a delayed board meeting!'

Exerting tight control upon panic-stricken nerves, Catriona hurried through reception, tapped lightly upon the office door, then nerved herself to enter the lion's den. He was working at his desk, simultaneously scribbling notes and dictating into a recorder. Without raising his head he waved her towards a chair, then humilitatingly ignored her presence while he resumed instant concentration, glancing through sheafs of government directives, at the same time taking notes and dictating replies to questions on a totally different subject. She could almost hear his brain humming as she sat tense, fists clenched tightly in her lap, mentally rearranging her erroneous impression of drawling Texans prone to lying lazily as cattle under a tree, chewing cud, contemplating nothing in particular.

She had become lulled into an attitude of mild complacency, exploring with her eyes his mane of russet-red hair—spark-flecked where a spotlight was raying down upon one temple—swept back from a formidable brow scored deep with concentration, wondering whether hooded eyes were slumbrous or flaring danger-bright, when he flung down his pen to address her sharply.

'Now, Miss Dunross, I'm ready to listen to whatever excuse you've cooked up for your late arrival.'

Her absorption was so complete that when he snapped his words she jerked so violently that her skirt rode up, exposing a glimpse of thigh and a pair of smooth rounded knees. Almost as a reflex action she jerked the hem downwards, and immediately regretted providing extra ammunition for his sarcastic tongue.

'Calm down,' he mocked coldly, giving her no time to reply to his accusation. 'Obviously you're mindful of the basic Muslim rule that whatever a man can see he's allowed to touch. However, as I live by the maxim, "To everything there is a season and a time to every purpose under the heaven" your attempted switch-off was unnecessary. My only pressing need at this moment is for a secretary to be available when she's needed, one who can be relied upon to turn up on time whatever the vagaries of the weather.'

Catriona had fully intended to apologise for her late arrival even though it was no fault of her own, had even been prepared to grovel slightly in spite of the fact that no reasonable person in possession of the salient facts could condemn her for being involved in an accident, but in spite of her good resolutions she responded to his verbal scratch with an aggravated spit.

'I thought we'd agreed that I was to be treated in exactly the same way as you would treat a male secretary, Mr Casson,' she rose to her feet to glower. 'That's hardly the type of dialogue one would expect to hear directed towards a male employee! If ever we're to achieve a satisfactory working partnership, I suggest you try avoiding the sex-object syndrome which is destructive of men and women as individuals and creates hostility between people who, given the chance to forget that they are each members of a different sex, might manage to work together quite amicably. Here and now, I would like to draw the line our relationship is to take, Mr Casson. While some women may appreciate the elemental-caveman, swinging-super-stud approach, I would very much prefer to be excluded from the "Me Tarzan ... You Jane" type of situation!' Trembling as near as she dared towards the dumbfounded beast whose fangs she had so savagely drawn, she scrutinised his heavily-leaden desk and said coolly, 'And now, acting upon the premise that silence may be taken for consent, I intend starting work. If you would be good enough to indicate the pile of correspondence to which replies have been dictated . . .?'

Though she was quaking in her shoes she betrayed no inkling, not even when, with a hissed-in breath of astonishment, he uncoiled from his seat and stalked around the desk to tower above the flaxen plait pinned into an elegant coil on top of her defiantly tilted head.

'Brave words, Miss Dunross,' he threatened with thinly concealed anger, 'wisely directed from behind a palisade of petticoats, for, as I'm certain you've realised, if a man had dared speak to me in such a manner I would have rewarded his gall with a sock in the jaw!'

She blanched from the suspicion that, with temper aroused, he was quite capable of taking her at her word by treating her as he would another man, and felt only slightly reassured when he continued with deadly deliberation, 'I would be well within my rights to dismiss you for impertinence, but that would be taking the easy way out, and far less satisfying than ensuring that you're made to work out your contract until either I grow tired of the novelty of taming a vixen, or you come crawling on your belly begging to be released!'

For the following two hours Catriona worked steadily through a pile of work left neglected for weeks because of Leon Casson's stubborn determination to mark time until his personnel department had managed to find a replacement for the comparatively rare male of the species who, as well as being a capable assistant, was also proficient in the twin arts of shorthand and typing. But as she dealt swiftly and efficiently with letters dictated on to tapes and relayed through an earpiece in a crisp, authoritative tone that kept her nerve ends quivering, one part of her mind remained numb, shocked by the impact of a threat delivered with such confidence she had been left in no doubt that it had been meant.

'Would you care to join me for lunch?'

Catriona raised dazed eyes towards the door and saw Sandra teetering on the threshold, her expression enquiring.

'Lunch?' she echoed with a puzzled frown.

'Exactly,' Sandra nodded, 'the practice of eating

a midday meal that's been indulged in by humans since the dawn of time.'

Catriona glanced from the sheaf of reports, letters and memos she had typed to two spools of tape remaining as yet untouched. 'I'd better not,' she murmured. 'But if it wouldn't be too much trouble, perhaps you could fetch me a sandwich and a glass of milk?'

'Now look here,' the young receptionist advanced farther into the room. 'Just because our boss exercises his brain, body and vocal chords constantly for up to fourteen hours a day there's no reason to suppose that his employees are expected to follow his example. You look drained,' she stated with the candour of youth, 'you must take a break or you'll burn yourself out and be completely useless tomorrow.'

'I suppose that makes sense.' Reluctantly, Catriona pushed back her chair and prepared to abandon her typewriter. 'I'll join you for a quick bite,' she glanced at her watch, 'but I mustn't be away any longer than half an hour.' Sandra led the way teetering on high heels along village 'streets' thronged with lunchtime strollers.

'Mealtimes are staggered,' she chatted pleasantly, guiding Catriona inside a large cafeteria-styled restaurant, 'consequently, the catering staff is never overstretched and one can always be sure of a vacant table. Yes, there's one!' She stood on tiptoe to peer above the heads of engrossed diners. 'Quick, Catriona, you stake a claim to it while I organise the nosh. I'm having steak and salad—what would you like, the menu's right there behind you?'

'Salad will do fine,' Catriona nodded, backing towards the vacant table, 'but not steak, I'd prefer an omelette, please, if there is one.'

Breathless with haste, she successfully secured the table and sank into a chair to gaze with wide, wondering eyes around the tastefully furnished, spotlessly clean interior with a counter ranged along the full length of one wall behind which chefs wearing tall white hats were busy preparing meals to be dished out to the waiting queue by waitresses dressed in the same crisp, colourful gingham that had been used to make napkins placed upright in a glass in the middle of each table, and curtains looped on to poles by brass rings, draping half the length of plate glass windows.

Lampshades, evocative of dainty lace-trimmed mobcaps, were hanging level with air vents and bobbing in the draught, creating an impression of a bevy of old ladies bending inquisitive heads over each of the tables.

'Ham omelette suit you all right?' Sandra dumped a loaded tray on to the table and pushed a large dinner plate wholly covered with a succulent-looking omelette, and an accompanying dish of salad, towards her.

'I couldn't possibly eat all that,' she gasped, 'there must be enough there for four!'

'Try,' Sandra grinned, passing over rolls and butter. 'The meals are so good here that the only complaint one ever hears is a fear of becoming overweight. The company does us proud, meals are free and you can eat as much as you like—one glutton of my acquaintance managed to down four T-bone steaks at one sitting, but not a comment was made, not so much as an eyebrow raised by the catering manager.'

Catriona tried a portion of omelette—perfectly cooked, crisp around the edges, runny in the middle and stuffed generously with diced ham—and savoured it slowly. 'Mmm ... delicious!' she responded to Sandra's look of enquiry. 'If all the meals are as good as this then I'm certain to enjoy working here.'

Well satisfied with her reaction, Sandra turned her attention upon the largest steak Catriona had ever seen.

'Texas size,' Sandra grinned, correctly interpreting her expression. 'Everything here is geared to suit our boss and his Yankee contemporaries who like their steaks the way they like their women—attractive to look at, sizzling hot, and very satisfying! How did you get on with Leo, by the way!'

Sensing that the question was far less casual than it sounded, Catriona prevaricated. 'We hardly had time to exchange conversation—he was late for a board meeting, I believe.'

Sandra hastened to put her in the picture. 'He can be a bit overpowering at first, but you're sure to fall in love with him eventually, everyone does.'

With a forkful of food raised halfway to her lips Catriona hesitated, then returned the food to her plate, her appetite suddenly diminished.

'They do!'

'Oh, yes,' Sandra nodded, tucking into her steak with evident enjoyment. 'I did myself—still could, in fact, given the slightest hint of encouragement. It took me ages to come to terms with the fact that Leo is right out of my league,' she shrugged, 'and after all, I ask myself, why should he look twice at a tame kitten when his area of the woods is overrun with experienced felines who can give him more of a run for his money? Rumour has it that he has a room reserved permanently in a large hotel on the mainland to which he retreats whenever he feels an urge to return to civilisation and that he seldom goes there alone. Yet if we were to believe every female who's boasted that she's been favoured with an invitation, then all I can say is that our boss must rate high as a super-stud!'

Striving to be fair, Catriona swallowed her disgust and suggested gently, 'It seems a pity to judge a man simply on hearsay. If, as you say, you're not personally acquainted with any of the girls who've supposedly been his companions on illicit weekends, isn't it just possible that he's unfortunate enough to have become the target of malicious gossip?'

To Sandra's credit, she did not immediately disagree but hesitated, knife and fork poised above her plate, looking thoughtful. But then she shook her head, as if definitely making up her mind.

'No, if everything that's been said were mere speculation the rumours would have died a natural death by this time. Also, there's the fact that with my very own eyes I've seen girls coming out of his trailer-home at a very late—or rather, early hour of the morning. Our Leon is very definitely a rake,' she sighed a trifle enviously, 'but a gentlemanly rake who goes to great lengths to protect a girl's reputation. In a way, I'm glad I settled for Gordon—my boy-friend,' she enlightened in response to Catriona's look of enquiry. 'He's a deep sea diver, based on oil rig Lion, miles from here in the middle of the North Sea.'

Glad to get away from the subject of the boss she was beginning to dislike more and more with each passing hour, Catriona encouraged sympathetically. 'It must be a rather unsatisfactory courtship, you being here and your boy-friend so far away?'

For a second Sandra's youthful face clouded, then as if buoyed by renewed hope, immediately brightened.

'In one respect it is, in another it isn't,' she dimpled, then giggled a trifle shyly. 'During the fortnightly intervals while he's away I keep up my spirits by reminding myself that most of his very high earnings, as well as my own, are accumulating into a very nice nest egg which we intend using to set ourselves up in a small business once we're married. We've reckoned it'll take us another year at least to save sufficient capital, but meanwhile,' Catriona was surprised to see her blush, 'during the time he's allowed ashore Gordon devotes all his energies to compensating for his absence. He's loving, attentive, and unlike the majority of divers, perfectly content to remain faithful to one girl. Most of the divers, once they come ashore, can't wait to spend every penny they've earned, few of them have managed to maintain a stable home life, and their penchant for fast cars and even faster women is notorious. The very fact that they've chosen to take up such a dangerous form of employment indicates that they're adventurous, courageous, strong-willed characters who are consequently difficult to organise and control. They live and work under contant strain, hence their tendency to let off steam whenever they have the opportunity, yet according to Gordon they make marvellous workmates, dedicated types who, in spite of their reckless behaviour—it's been proved that the most dangerous pieces of apparatus in the hands of a diver are the motor-car and motor-cycle—look after one another to a degree normal workmen couldn't begin to comprehend. For instance, if one diver should go down alone he's liable to break every rule in the book. But if two divers go down together one will not allow the other to break a single rule. Such denizens of the deep are entitled to expect a modicum of tolerance from ordinary mortals, don't you agree?' she appealed, looking dreamily besotted.

Denizen of the deep! Catriona jerked, startled by the effect of a phrase that had immediately called to mind an image of Leon Casson, an ex-diver who fitted the designation as closely as he would fit into a wet suit—an alien to the island, an invader who threatened to disrupt her well organised life, a strange animal struggling with the problem of adjusting his wild spirit to a peaceful environment!

As if a warning growl had sounded in her ear, she glanced at her watch, then pushed her plate away.

'I must get back to work, Sandra, there's still reams of typing to do. The meal was delicious, thank you so much for keeping me company.'

'But you haven't finished it!' Sandra's astonished eyes swept over Catriona's half-empty plate, the untouched roll and small pat of butter. 'Obviously you're a glutton for work, but certainly not for food.

Still,' she sighed, then flashed a cheery grin, 'there isn't a secretary working here at base who wouldn't forgo meals for a week if it meant she was to be favoured with the chance of working in close contact with our rugged, very attractive boss. They're all livid, you know.' This remark stopped Catriona in her tracks just as she was about to take her leave.

'Livid about what?' she asked blankly.

'About the fact that you've managed to snatch *the* plum job right from under their noses. Every one of the base secretaries would have applied for the position as Leo's secretary, but, as he's always previously refused to even consider employing a female, no one bothered. You can imagine the fluttering it caused in the hen coop,' she chuckled, stabbing her fork into a piece of steak, 'when the news broke that a girl had been brought over from the mainland to fill the post they all coveted. It's even been suggested,' she directed a sly peep from beneath lowered lashes, 'that behind Leo's change of heart lurks an ulterior motive. *Were* you and he close friends before he offered you the job, Catriona?' she urged, obviously agog with curiosity. 'You can trust me with the truth, I promise I won't tell a soul!'

Catriona stared, appalled. Too angry to excuse Sandra's tactlessness on the grounds of extreme youth, or even to acknowledge that the girl's question had probably been prompted by others, she blazed,

'No, we most certainly were not!' Directing a look that made Sandra feel humble as a peasant in the presence of offended royalty, she iced disdainfully, 'The truth which you seem so anxious to establish is this: I took the job as secretary to Leon Casson because I had no choice, but had I met the man first, nothing on earth would have induced me to agree to working with such a moronic, self-opinionated, arrogantly conceited beast!'

Not until she whirled away from the table did she become conscious of the concentrated hush that had fallen over the cafeteria. Not so much as a tinkle of cutlery, the chink of glass, the rattle of plates, disturbed the breath-held silence of fascinated diners, whose attention was trained upon the girl whose ringing outburst had coincided with the appearance of the man standing framed in the doorway behind her. Warned by some instinct, she spun on her heel to face the bleak, inscrutable, yet somehow menacing features of Leon Casson.

Stunned, as much by her own uncharacteristic loss of control as by his unexpected presence, she froze, prepared to be castigated, and almost wished she had been when, instead of the public rebuke their audience was obviously expecting, he stepped aside to permit her exit with an audible, polite murmur.

'Ah, Miss Dunross, I thought I might find you here. Did you enjoy your lunch?'

She managed a nod, then swept past him with her head held high, feeling completely out-gunned, out-manoeuvred—chastised as an ill-mannered child.

Amber-flecked eyes seemed to be boring into her back all the way to the office, so she was not altogether unprepared for the snarl that erupted the moment she stepped inside and heard the door slammed shut when he stalked in behind her.

'What the devil do you mean by airing your opinion of my character before half of my employees?' he blasted. 'You may type faster than most men, Miss Dunross, might even excel in efficiency, but there are two assets valuable in a private secretary that you appear to be lacking—discretion, and a sense of loyalty!'

Knowing that his criticism was justified, she hung her head and without turning round apologised stiffly,

'I'm sorry, I had no right to say what I did, the only excuse I can offer is that I was provoked.'

He pounced, sending a shudder of fright through her slender frame. 'I'm in no mood to listen to trivial excuses. And don't stand there like a snivelling schoolgirl, look at me when I'm speaking to you!'

His shot touched flame to her powder-keg pride, spinning her round with head held erect, flashing sparks of antagonism from eyes green as the seas washing the shores of her island home. Her lips parted to spill words of resentment boiling lava-hot inside of her, then froze into a gape when he beat her to it with a spate of cold indictment.

'I've just finished interviewing the driver of the car in which you travelled to work this morning, and while doing so I managed to elicit the information that it was you and not he who was behind the wheel when the car was damaged. I also learned that you were fully aware that it's strictly forbidden for anyone not oficially appointed to take charge of a company car. Rules, however trivial they may sometimes appear, are drawn up for a specific purpose. The rule in question is no exception, and because it was ignored the company is now faced with the expense of repairing the car—an obligation which normally would have been met by our insurance company. As I can see no reason why I should overlook deliberate insubordination, and bearing in mind, Miss Dunross, your request to be treated with the same degree of privilege as any male employee, I've decided that both culprits are equally to blame and have consequently instructed that a proportionate amount of money is to be deducted from each of your salaries until the debt has been discharged!'

CHAPTER FIVE

'PUT those away this minute!' Aunt Hanna directed sharply when Catriona, dressed in faded denims and an ancient checked blouse salvaged from the bottom of a pile of jumble, appeared in the living-room clutching a handful of paintbrushes. 'You've been working hard as any slave these past weeks, arriving home at ungodly hours of the night too tired to enjoy your dinner, fit only to drop into bed exhausted! I insist that you relax and try to unwind now that you've finally been allowed a day off. That boss of yours must be an absolute monster!' she burst out indignantly, enraged by the sight of a pale, peaked face and eyes green as troubled seas made to look enormous by bruising shadows of fatigue.

'He's not solely to blame.' In spite of her antagonism, her escalating dislike of the man who for the past three weeks had seemed to go out of his way to make her life unbearable, Catriona strove to be fair. 'Because of a continuing glut of oil and falling prices, a directive was issued from head office stating that a second look had to be taken at the economics of running both the land base and offshore rigs. Cutting costs turned out to be a major problem. Small economies suggested by heads of departments helped to some extent, but as one man pointed out, the rate of inflation is such that small savings are swallowed up before any benefits can accrue. After a series of discussions, it was finally agreed that any major improvements would have to be gained from trimming the enormous outlay expended upon the oil rigs themselves, consequently,' she sighed, her brain still reeling from the effect of having concentrated for hours upon the avalanche of figures, facts and statistics that had cascaded on to her desk, 'a schedule of twelve-hour day, working a seven-day week, became unavoidable.'

'Humph!' her aunt snorted, 'and I suppose now that you've both been driven into the ground with exhaustion, your boss has relented by deciding—too late, in my opinion—that you deserve a break?'

'Exhaustion,' Catriona echoed hollowly, 'is a word long since deleted from his vocabulary. The man is a phenomenon, Aunt, a human powerhouse who seems to delight in running shock waves down the spines of every one of his employees.'

'But he *has* allowed you this weekend off,' her aunt insisted, unable to suppress a grudging admiration for the captain of industry.

Catriona shook her head. 'I'm afraid he didn't,' she confessed, looking momentarily hunted. 'As I felt on the verge of collapse, I sneaked out of the office last night while his attention was diverted and before he had a chance to mention working over the weekend. I suppose, if the truth were known, I'm actually playing hookey.'

'And about time, too,' the old lady defended warmly. 'Hard work is not a curse, but drudgery certainly is! And what about that young man of yours, he's bound to be feeling neglected?'

'Young man?' Catriona queried absently, her

thought, still confined within the office that lately had taken on the appearance of a prison cell. 'Oh, my young man!' With a guilty blush she jerked back to earth. 'No, he hasn't complained, fortunately, he's been kept as frantically busy as I have.'

'Then when do I get to meet him?' her aunt persisted doggedly, then stirred panic in Catriona's breast by sniffing with more than a hint of acidity, 'If I hear any more excuses for his absence I shall be tempted to think that he's non-existent. It's not natural,' she snorted, 'for a man to put up with long separations from the girl he loves, especially when they're both confined within the same small island.'

Scouring her tired brain for inspiration, Catriona laid the paintbrushes aside and played for time by picking up the teapot, then stalling as long as she dared over pouring out a cupful and diluting its strength by adding sugar and milk to the dark, strong brew. Finally, unnerved by her aunt's unswerving stare, she forced herself to lie,

'But we see each other every day. Didn't I tell you that we work together in the same office?'

'No, you did not.' Her aunt's face cleared. 'You merely mentioned that he's an American ex-diver promoted against his inclinations to a position too exalted to allow him to feel comfortable in humble surroundings. Is that why you're so eager to begin painting?' she condemned with a return of her earlier sharpness. 'Have you deliberately omitted to invite him here because you're ashamed of your home?'

The sight of wrinkled skin tightening around lips compressed to hide their quivering drove Catriona to her feet.

'Of course not, Aunt Hanna, how could you think such a thing?' Then, feeling the panic of a swimmer dragged out of her depth by a relentless undertow, she struck out blindly. 'He has a standing invitation to call whenever he can manage it—which who knows might even be today!'

'Today . . .!' The old lady's frail, rounded shoulders squared erect. 'Then why ever didn't you say so, girl?' she gasped. 'I'd better begin preparing a meal for three just in case!'

When she began clearing the breakfast dishes, moving around the table with a spring in her step and a pleased smile playing around her mouth before disappearing into the kitchen with her tray, Catriona forced her leaden limbs to move, but kept her mind blank, refusing to dwell upon the inevitable outcome of her deception, yet nurturing a hope too faint to bear close inspection that somehow, from somewhere, she would find a solution to her dilemma.

She had taken down the curtains, removed ornaments and pictures from the walls, and was struggling to shift heavier items of furniture into the middle of the room when she heard her aunt's voice drifting from the direction of the small kitchen jutting like an afterthought from the rear of the cottage. She paused in her task of inching a heavy oak dresser, one side at a time, away from the wall to cock an attentive ear, then smiled when a draught of cool air fanned her cheek, imagining her aunt engaged in her usual altercation with a bad-tempered, permanently peckish gander that had formed a habit of begging at the kitchen door.

Wishing she had not succumbed to the lazy luxury

of leaving her long golden hair unconfined, flowing freely over her shoulders, she tossed a heavy strand back before bending to resume her struggle with the cumbersome dresser, then froze, shocked into immobility by a response that in no way resembled the hiss of a hungry gander but sounded more of an aggravated growl.

'Good morning, ma'am, I believe Miss Catriona Dunross lives here? Would you be good enough to tell her that Leon Casson would like a word?'

Not even in her worst nightmares had she experienced the sort of dialogue that followed so swiftly she had no time to intervene.

'You sound like an American,' Aunt Hanna decided triumphantly. 'You must be Kate's boyfriend, you fit her description exactly. I'm Hanna Dunross. Kate's aunt—come along in, Mr Casson. I've waited such a long time to meet the man who's managed to entice my niece away from her beloved university!'

Heavily shod feet advancing across the stone-flagged kitchen floor sent a presentiment of doom quivering along Catriona's stiff spine. Slowly she straightened and looked up, just in time to see a look of puzzlement replacing the frown of displeasure on Leon Casson's face as he sauntered into the living-room. Instinct warned her that a disclaimer was trembling on his lips when he turned to slew her aunt a look of grave apology.

'I'm afraid, Miss Dunross, there's been some——'

'Leon *darling*, what a wonderful surprise!' Casting caution to the winds, Catriona flung herself at her boss with arms open wide. 'I know you promised you'd come today if you could, but I never dared hope that you'd manage to get away!' Sledgehammer heartbeats pounded in her ears as she spun within the loose circle of his arms to direct a blushing, feverishly-bright appeal to her aunt. 'There now, didn't I warn you that Leon might turn up today?'

'Indeed you did, Kate dear,' her aunt glowed, beaming her approval of the rangy, russet-maned male who had roared up to her door like a lion but who now seemed as tongue-tied as a bewildered lamb. 'No need to feel shy, young man,' she chuckled, 'sit down and make yourself at home. I believe you Americans are fond of coffee—I'd better make sure we have some.'

Feeling mauled by a grip that descended upon her waist the moment she tried to slink away, Catriona lifted mutely appealing eyes to his face, unashamedly begging, prepared to grovel if only he would promise not to give her away. For one heartstopping moment he seemed about to insist upon explaining the true situation, but then, with a glint in his eyes that boded ill for the future, he veered from the impulse to destroy an old lady's very obvious happiness.

'Thank you, ma'am,' he drawled, stepping aside to allow her access into the kitchen, 'a cup of coffee would be very acceptable.'

Catriona sagged with relief, amazed by his uncharacteristic consideration, but was not surprised when immediately the door had closed behind her aunt's sprightly figure he swiftly reverted to normal.

'So you're the one who's been spreading the

rumour that you and I share more than a boss and employee relationship!' he accused, stalking the tiny living-room as if it were a cage. 'You're just like the rest of your sex, who flock to work with the oil companies motivated by the hope of finding a husband! The realisation that most oil men are happily married is not slow to register, then life is turned into a competition to see who can successfully manage to sink their claws into the few eligible men left available!'

'How dare you imply that I'm some sort of huntress in search of game!' she choked indignantly. 'I realise that in this instance appearances are against me, but I assure you I wouldn't dream of gossiping about my affairs to fellow workers—and as for rumours running rife around the base, it appears to me that one who's worked so hard to build up a rakish reputation ought not to be surprised to discover that his motives are often suspect so far as any member of the opposite sex is concerned. In other words, Mr Casson, your own amorous adventures, both past and present, give rise to speculation about any female unfortunate enough to have to work in your proximity!'

'Have you ever stopped to consider that my *amorous adventures* could be as imaginary as your own, Miss Dunross?' he hissed, mindful of the need to keep his voice lowered. 'That there might be other females beside yourself who derive a vicarious thrill from casting themselves in the role of *femme fatale* with myself an unwilling Lothario?'

'I did no such thing!' she denied, crimson-cheeked. 'There's a very simple explanation for my . . . er . . .'

'Lies . . .?' he suggested coldly.

'Harmless deception,' she corrected with a proud tilt of her chin. 'I need hardly point out that my aunt is elderly, hard of hearing, and almost blind, and she's therefore in no condition to be left to live alone. But as she also possesses more than her fair share of Sheltie independence and pride, I had to find some convincing excuse for leaving my job at university and returning to Shetland to work for the oil company. When she jumped to the conclusion that I'd fallen in love with some man working on the base the notion seemed too heavensent to deny, so in order to keep her mind at rest I played along.'

He stopped prowling and halted in the centre of the room to observe her closely. Bravely she withstood his laser-cold stare, wondering at his talent for attracting attention, at the way he dominated the centre stage with one economical movement, a terse statement.

'You still haven't explained why you singled me out for the dubious honour of being named as your consort.'

'I didn't,' she stated simply, 'I merely drew upon my imagination for a description, lurid, dramatic, exaggerated enough to satisfy my aunt's secret passion for brutal males—if you recall, it was she who decided that my description fitted you to perfection.'

'Are you being sarcastic, Miss Dunross?' The threat contained within his soft drawl was unmistakable. Feeling her knees beginning to tremble, Catriona turned away and on the pretext of searching for a duster managed to conceal the effects of a heart drumming a warning to retreat. Foolishly, she ignored its message.

'I've often thought it strange,' she tilted, chancing a sideways look through the golden veil of hair that had fallen across her cheek, 'that people who are prone to resorting to sarcasm seem quick to attribute their vice to others. I never indulge in sarcasm, Mr Casson; only occasionally in wit.'

'In that case you would be well advised to be very careful how you handle it.' His dark brown sweater made a perfect foil for eyes glinting sharp as amber chips as he strolled towards her. 'Wit is a dangerous dagger, the only weapon with which—when wielded by a novice—it's possible to stab oneself in the back!'

She lifted a hand to riffle nervous fingers through her hair when his threat registered. How foolish she had been to antagonise the man instead of pleading for his co-operation! If it were only her own welfare that was at stake she would have seen him in hell before choking back her pride, but for the sake of her aunt's happiness she clenched her teeth and forced herself to flatter his enormous conceit.

'You wouldn't deliberately shatter an old lady's illusions?' she asked, projecting a look of helpless appeal, hoping to find a soft spot in his tough hide. 'I've often heard it said that Texans have hearts as wide and generous as the prairies.'

She held her breath and waited for his reaction, then felt a leap of triumph when, after seconds spent impaled by his rapier-sharp glance, she saw his lips quirk in to a smile.

'I'll co-operate with you, Miss Dunross,' he conceded lightly, 'although it goes against the grain to deceive an old lady who has impressed me as being a person of high integrity. But "nuthin' is done for nuthin' " as they say in my country—I'll play ball with you only if you'll agree to join in the game.'

'I don't understand,' she stared perplexed. 'All I'm asking you to do is pretend that we're friends for the duration of a coffee break! Once you've left the house there's no reason why you and my aunt should ever meet again.'

'That would be rather a shame, don't you think?' His effrontery took her breath away. 'Your aunt and I enjoyed instant rapport, I'm sure she's looking forward just as much as I am to furthering our acquaintance.'

'Don't be ridiculous,' she gasped, discarding her cloak of diplomacy. 'I'll think up some feasible excuse for your future non-appearance—imply that we've fallen out of love, or something, and that you've left the island—that way, I'll be able to continue living at home without need for further deception.'

'No,' much to her amazement he shook his head, 'that course of action doesn't fit in with my plans.'

'Your plans!' she glared, unconsciously clenching her fists. 'Your plans have nothing whatsoever to do with me!'

'The ball game, remember, Miss Dunross?' he smiled unpleasantly. 'Far from wanting our mythical friendship dissolved, I've decided that it would suit me fine if it should continue, indeed, even blossom into an engagement. With you posing as my fiancée—a sort of decoy duck to draw the attention of the gossips—I should come under much less closer surveillance. As you can imagine, life in a close-knit community such as exists at the camp is made tedious by lack of privacy, so much so that at times I feel I'm living in a glasshouse, its walls lined with peering, inquisitive female faces. I suppose being a dedicated bachelor makes such speculative interest inevitable. However, as a man's rating drops immediately he is removed from the marriage market, I reckon that a presentable, undemanding fiancée should provide an excellent screen to protect my private activities. So consider yourself engaged, Miss Dunross—I'd better get used to calling you Kate— immediately an opportunity presents itself I'll buy you a ring.'

The thought of being linked in any way, and however temporarily, to the most aggravatingly chauvinistic male ever to trespass into her own private vicinity caused her a visible, distasteful squirm.

'I'm sorry, Mr Casson——'

'Leon,' he corrected firmly.

'. . . such a scheme is totally unacceptable to me,' she continued stiffly, ignoring his interruption. 'In fact the suggestion is so outrageous I'm tempted to believe you're enjoying a private joke at my expense. If you don't mind,' she stood aside, 'I'd like you to go now. Don't bother taking leave of my aunt, I'll make your apologies and explain that a suddenly remembered appointment made it necessary for you to leave in a hurry.'

The tinkle of a spoon in a saucer, the rattle of cups and the shuffling sound of slippered feet progressing across the kitchen floor seemed to indicate that her directive had been issued too late. She stiffened, then when the door latch lifted winged an unconscious look of pleading in his direction.

'Make up your mind quickly,' he hissed, deliberately holding her to ransom, 'either do as I ask, or resign yourself to the inevitability of having to confess to your aunt that you lied!'

He strode to open the door, obviously intent upon assisting the old lady at the other side, and was ready to pull it ajar before Catriona's numbed brain responded to the need for action.

'Very well,' she spat resentment of his dominance, her bitter reluctance to acknowledge that he held the whip hand, 'I appear to have no choice. But I promise you I'll take advantage of every opportunity to make you regret forcing me to submit to barbaric blackmail!'

He flung the door wide. 'That coffee sure smells good, Miss Dunross!' His calm indifference to her threat was emphasised by a carefree smile, by the casual, almost lazy ease with which he relieved her aunt of a tray laden with coffee pot, mugs and a plateful of homemade scones.

'You're a real gentleman, Mr Casson,' her aunt beamed, happily relinquishing her burden to take her place at the table. 'I'm sorry the place is in such a mess.' Her displeased glance roved the bare walls, curtainless window frames and disturbed furniture. 'Kate couldn't wait to begin doing the place up in preparation for your first visit, yet I felt certain, from the little she had told me about you, that you were not the type of man to notice a few patches of paintless woodwork.'

'Quite right, Miss Dunross,' he approved, 'Kate is

inclined to worry too much over trifles. And by the way,' he continued, so casually the impact of his words almost passed over Catriona's head, 'perhaps now that your niece and I have agreed to make our engagement official, you wouldn't mind dropping the Mr and calling me Leon?'

'You're *engaged*! Kate, is this true?'

Faced with an aunt almost beside herself with joy, Catriona could manage no more than a blushing nod.

'Oh, child, I'm so happy for you!' She flung up her arms in the air. 'Happy for you both!' Her glance swung towards Leon and lingered as if anxious to commit to memory the features of the first male to enter their circle for many years.

'I take it that you approve, then, Aunt Hanna?' he teased, displaying an audacious charm that left Catriona fuming.

'Approve?' Her voice quavered as if she were very close to tears. 'My dear young man, I'm delighted! Kate has shown so little interest in finding a husband I was beginning to worry that she might finish up wearing a bonnet with strings tied beneath her chin!'

Hastily, with colour rioting in her cheeks, Catriona endeavoured to distract his attention from a remark he obviously found puzzling.

'Sugar ... er ... Leon? Do try a scone.' She pushed the plate nearer towards him. 'Aunt Hanna's famous for her baking.'

But as she had feared, his curiosity had been aroused—even increased—by her own heightened colour.

'And does a bonnet with strings tied beneath the chin hold some special significance?' he prodded gently.

'It hasn't now, but it used to when I was a girl,' Aunt Hanna laughed. 'In the old days, a woman who bought a bonnet with satin-faced ribbons attached to tie beneath the chin was resigning herself to the fact that her youth was over. Every mother, whatever her age, once her second child was born, exchanged her hat for a bonnet with ties. A spinster, however, could flaunt in her hat for much longer because as long as she was wearing one any bachelor might pluck up courage to "speer" her, and if she was already keeping company she could continue wearing her hat until she was a "bittock" of thirty— but no longer, otherwise she ran the risk of being regarded as a figure of fun, of being told to stop "gallivanting about wi' a hat, and dress as a decent woman should, in a bonnet with ties".

'I don't believe it!' Casting Catriona a look of delighted amusement, Leon threw back his head and laughed aloud.

'I hope you realise, Kate,' he eventually managed to tease with a wicked twinkle in his tawny-cat's eyes, 'that marriage to me will save you from the ignominy of a tombstone that does *not* read: "beloved wife of . . ." '

Incensed to the point of slaying him where he sat, she trembled to her feet, determined to confess to deceit, to rid herself of the necessity to pretend a liking for the man who possessed more power to infuriate than any other of her acquaintance. But as if sensing her objective he rose from his chair before she could speak closed in to tower over her.

'Dear Kate,' he reproved, swooping to place a silencing kiss upon her shocked mouth, 'in the excitement of the moment I forgot my original reason for coming here. I have to fly out to the rig and I need you with me. Don't bother to change, we'll be travelling by 'copter, so you'll be kept cosy and warm in your survival suit!'

CHAPTER SIX

THE din being caused by rotor blades whirling just above their heads, together with vibrations juddering through the length of the small two-seater helicopter, made normal speech impossible. Catriona sat tense, barely conscious of straps holding her tightly into her seat, gripped by the fascinating terror of soaring like a bird, an infinitesimal speck in an endless stretch of sky, lifted by air currents, jolted by turbulence, skimming one moment low enough to make her toes curl with fear of sudden immersion in grey, foam-flecked waves, the next whooshing swiftly as a lift to the height of a multi-storey building.

'Are you frightened?' Leon yelled, leaning sideways to distract her wide, fixed stare away from the transparent dome that made her feel encapsulated within a fragile glass bubble.

'No,' she mouthed, then vigorously shook her head.

And in a curious way she was not, for in spite of the noise filling the flimsy structure of a craft so small she felt exceedingly vulnerable, she was experiencing no panic, had the utmost confidence in the brown, sinewed hands so capably manipulating the controls.

He had hustled her out of the house so quickly she had had little time to protest, to think, or even to do more than gasp a garbled explanation to her astonished aunt.

'We'll be back before nightfall, Miss Dunross,' Leon had yelled above the revving engine of his silver Range Rover, 'keep dinner hot for us, I'm looking forward to some real home cooking!'

Catriona strained her ears when once more he shouted above the noise of the engine. 'This is an expensive way to commute, maybe, but to come by boat would take us twenty-four hours. If you look closely, you can just see the outline of the rig appearing on the horizon!'

She leant forward to peer into misty oblivion and at first could see nothing, then as her eyes became adjusted she spotted a bulky outline in the far distance which gradually solidified as they drew nearer into an enormous superstructure perched on four concrete legs, with two huge steel-girdered towers poking upwards as if sending a message of defiance to a lowering sky. Seconds later she was able to distinguish the shapes of cranes, masses of pipework, ducting, steel stairways connecting the lower, middle and upper decks of the man-made marvel that looked like a ship afloat with lifeboats attached to each deck, but which was actually a miniature town set on massive concrete legs with a framework of steel girders keeping it anchored firmly to the sea-bed.

Rooted to immobility by a mixture of fascination and fear, she stared downward while Leon, responding to instructions crackling through a radio receiver, hovered above the rig, then began lowering the craft towards a tiny square landing pad ringed like a target that appeared to her horrified eyes no larger than the area of paved yard behind her aunt's cottage. She glanced swiftly at Leon's face and saw that it was tense with concentration while slowly, as the screams of the engine and teeth-chattering vibrations intensified, he inched lower and lower until the craft touched down on to a surface covered with a tightly-stretched, open-weave rope carpet.

'Congratulations, you coped with the ordeal well,' Leon grinned as he cut the engine and eased a brace of earphone radio receivers from his head. 'One of my earlier assistants reacted like a quivering jellyfish to his first chopper flight out to the rig.'

She responded to the near-compliment with a blush, amazed by the warm glow of pleasure that encompassed her body as thoroughly as the bright orange survival suit, bagging around her ankles because the legs were too long, with a drawstring hood that could be tied beneath the chin and a full length zip which, when it was fastened, made her feel like an astronaut prepared to take her first steps on the moon.

The disguising effect of the suit was such that when she jumped gingerly down to the ground the man hurriedly approaching spared her no more than a cursory glance before striding past, making no effort to assist her.

'I'm glad you set off early, boss,' he called out to Leon as he jumped from the cockpit, 'we've just received a weather report warning that a force eight gale is imminent! How come,' he challenged cheerfully, his teeth flashing white against weather-browned skin, 'you always seem to manage to make an indefinite stay?'

'The weather in this region is so darned unpredictable that a settled twenty-four-hour spell is considered not far short of a miracle, and well you know it, you old roustabout,' Leon growled, before turning towards Catriona to effect an introduction. 'Kate,' his effrontery set her teeth on edge, 'I'd like you to meet Geoff Barclay, my installation manager!'

'Geoff,' he grinned, waiting narrow-eyed for his reaction, 'this is Miss Catriona Dunross, my new assistant and even newer fiancée!'

If Neptune himself had suddenly risen from the surrounding waves he could not have met with a more stunned, mouth-gaping reception. Seeming bereft of words, the manager stood staring fixedly at wind-whipped hair flaying silken lashes across Catriona's flushed cheeks and appeared for a moment to be in danger of suffering a fit of apoplexy. But when she stepped towards him with a hand outstretched and a smile pinned to her stiff lips his massive shoulders squared beneath a yellow oilskin jacket and a kindling of warmth appeared in eyes shaded by the brim of a protective helmet.

'Well, I'll be blowed!' She almost had to guess the words snatched from his lips by a stiff wind. 'I'm delighted to make your acquaintance, Miss Dunross!' Her hand became swallowed into his hearty clasp, then shaken until her arm felt like an ill-used pump handle. 'A woman aboard an oil rig is a rare sight indeed—usually the only birds we see are seagulls— but the news that the boss has finally branded himself a steer will cause more of a stir than a bleeding hurricane! Oh ... er ... begging your pardon, Miss Dunross, no offence meant, I'm sure.'

'Don't apologise, Kate wants no special privileges,'

Leon grunted, leading the way towards a flight of steps descending from the heli-pad to a deck below.' She insists that she's to be treated like just another guy—although as her fiancé I can't promise to follow her instructions to the letter,' he mocked, turning to flash her a wicked look. 'I'll leave it to you, Geoff, to explain the situation to the rest of the men. Tell them they're to carry on roughnecking as normal, that they've no need to curb their language or tone down their shouted abuses just because there's a woman aboard. In fact,' he instructed lightly, yet with a tight-lipped coolness that carried an unmistakable note of warning, 'be sure to make it plain that I shall be most annoyed if ever I'm given reason to suspect any one of them of treating my assistant in the way they're accustomed to treating young, attractive members of the opposite sex!'

Sensing the manager's sympathetic scrutiny, Catriona hid her mortified expression by staring straight ahead as she followed in Leon's wake, relieving some of her anger by spearing dagger sharp glances towards a spot sited between his shoulder-blades where, had her weapon been lethal, she could have inflicted mortal damage. Shaken by the strength of emotions he seemed to delight in arousing, she quickened her steps to keep up with his rapid descent of an iron stairway leading down to a deck resounding with noisy activity.

'Before calling a meeting of heads of staff, I'll take you on a quick tour of the rig,' he offered, halting at the foot of the steps to watch her hurried, breathless descent.

'Please don't put yourself out,' she declined swiftly,

'I'm sure you must have more important things to do. If I'm not needed for a while, I'll be perfectly happy exploring on my own.'

'If it didn't suit me I wouldn't offer to escort you,' he snapped, relieved of the need to impress an audience. 'The boss of an oil rig has the same responsibilities as the captain of a ship, inasmuch as he needs to be familiar with everything that's going on on board and to be seen to understand it.'

She ached to pull away from his grasp upon her elbow, but forced herself to appear unconcerned as he guided her closer to an area of frantic activity where a gang of men wearing protective helmets and filthy, mud-soaked boiler suits were turning, winching, screwing and positioning heavy items of engineering equipment, all of which were coated with the slippery black gold for which the treasure-hunting oil men seemed prepared to risk their lives.

'This is the drilling platform, the core of our operations,' he told her tersely. 'Extracting the oil and pumping it ashore goes on twenty-four hours a day. Other work, engineering hook-up, maintenance and overhaul, also carries on continuously. This rig does two jobs, collecting and storing oil from three other platforms as well as drilling and extracting its own oil from a reservoir below. That's the only reason we're here, to drill and produce oil, consequently the platform is never allowed to sleep.'

In spite of growing resentment of the bounty-hunting oil men who were despoiling and plundering her homeland as thoroughly as earlier Norse invaders, Catriona felt a stirring of respect for the sheer guts and determination being displayed by men eager to achieve their goal, who shrugged off the hardship of working in intolerable conditions, of being soaked to the skin, chilled to the bone, and made conscious each time they glanced upwards of a grey, angrily-heaving, icily-hostile sea.

Leon effected no further introductions to any of his tough, weatherbeaten personnel, but as they continued their tour of the rig she shrank from a battery of interested, lively, calculating, puzzled, anticipatory, and frankly flirtatious eyes that followed her progress past cranes unloading pipes and containers of food and materials from a supply boat anchored close by; through a galley preparing round-the-clock meals for an army of hungry men; around a power station big enough to light up a small town that had a desalinator to help out with the fresh water supply and a heating system to ensure that bedrooms and lounges were kept at a comfortable temperature; through a computer room monitoring information from hundreds of key instruments installed upon the rig and a laboratory where chemical checks were being made on the quality of the extracted oil.

Their final destination was an area filled with lines of pipework, and cement storage tanks. Leon paused to wave an encompassing arm. 'This is the heart of Oilfield Lion, into which oil is pumped from the other three platforms to be discharged, together with our own, a hundred and twenty miles under the sea to the terminal at base. There's more wealth flowing through here in a couple of hours than any one man could earn in an extended lifetime!'

Because of a smile that had appeared lurking

around his mouth immediately he had sensed discomfiture caused by eyes probing her nymphish curves and the feminine undulation of a walk emphasised rather than disguised by a survival suit usually worn by striding, muscular men, Catriona had begun dimly to suspect that she had been deliberately subjected not so much to a tour of inspection as a challenge to test her assertion that she could mix without embarrassment in the company of sex-hungry males. Consequently she was stung to scoff,

'Doesn't it bother you that while man may be coming first in the race for gold, Mother Nature is trailing last?'

'That remark is typical of the narrow attitude we oil men have come to expect from Shelties who, in common with the animals they breed, seem ever ready to snap at the hand that feeds them!'

As they glared mutual dislike across a narrow strip of gangway with just a stretch of metal railing marking the edge of a drop into a fermenting sea, she tried to persuade herself that the tingling that had begun in her ears and then spread slowly to every nerve end was due entirely to the perpetual high level of noise being emitted by heavy industrial machinery; that the fluttering in her stomach, the sensation of floating in the air with her feet far above the ground was the natural response of a body unused to continuous vibration and had no connection with a look of contempt in wild, tawny eyes or the derisive curl of lips which a lifetime ago had silenced her with a kiss that had been inflicted as a punishing stamp of authority, then had graduated into an exploring warmth that had melted through her crust of frozen resistance as persistently as a bee searches for honey.

'In spite of the fact that we've leant over backwards to meet terms that would have put Shylock to shame,' he continued angrily, 'you'd all like us banished as far out of sight as possible, still treat us as if we had horns jutting from our helmets like the invaders of long ago! After all, what did you have before we came to your island except solitude, isolation, and a precarious living dependent upon the caprice of herring shoals and the sale of Fair Isle woollens?'

Clinging to the railing as support against a gradually freshening wind that was already whipping spray on to the high top deck and churning the sea around the rig's massive concrete legs into a hissing, foam-flecked cauldron, Catriona released all of her storm-pent resentment.

'We had beautiful landscapes where now we have sludge tanks; misty sunlight in place of arc lamps, gambolling lambs, contented ponies, and a magnificent seabird population that's now threatened with extinction because of heavy, treacly oil being spilled into the Voe waters!'

'We've had *one* bad accident only!' he responded swiftly. 'Since then we've tightened up regulations regarding inspection and penalties for spillage to ensure that the same sort of incident can never happen again!'

'Have you ever seen an otter caught in an oil slick?' Deliberately she ignored his boast.

'Not since tankers have been refused entry to the

terminal whenever spotter planes have seen oil slicks behind them out at sea,' he replied with such calm reasonableness she suffered a stab of remorse. Yet in spite of his air of assurance—or maybe because of it—she refused to back down.

'Can you really be surprised at the attitude of islanders who've been forced to exchange peace of mind for a knife-edge situation in which more and more tankers will be prone to accidents during severe winter weather? If another calamity *should* occur, you oil men will discover to your cost that we Shetlanders haven't forgotten lessons learnt during hundreds of years of repelling "get rich quick and then run" invaders!'

The howling of the wind combined with the din of heavy machinery to form a crescendo of sound that made it necessary for him to grab her by the shoulders and jerk her forward until the hot breath of his temper was searing past her ear.

The line of his jaw seemed cast in bronze, his lips so tightly set words were ejected in a hiss.

'Reading legends about raping Norsemen is apt to make modern man envious of his less inhibited ancestors, but having made your acquaintance, Miss Dunross, I now have no difficulty in understanding why raiders who abducted women from these islands are reported by historians to have received medals for bravery!'

As if in sympathy with his sentiments, a howling streak of wind gusted powerful as a jet stream along the exposed gangway, shuddering across the corrugated wall of a workshop, catching Catriona's slender figure full force against her back so that she was flung forward and caught like a tattered flag against the bulwark of his rock-hard chest.

Immediately his arms whipped out to lash her tightly against his braced frame, and with a gasp of fear she grabbed hold of his jumper and buried her head against his shoulder until the demoniacal gust had passed. Seconds later she attempted to raise her head, but discovered that she was held fast, her head level with his chin, by a tangle of long tresses flung cloakwise across one broad shoulder. If he had not discarded his survival suit the problem would not have arisen, but as it was, spun gold strands were clinging to his sweater as if loath to let go, maintaining a determined hold even while she tugged and twisted in an effort to escape from the steady heartbeat pulsating against her cheek.

'I feel like a fly caught in a soft silken web,' Leon murmured with an undertone of laughter, sliding his palm across the nape of her neck with the obvious intention of sweeping his hand beneath the golden curtain to ease it from his shoulder. But immediately he made contact with smooth, warm skin upon a nape tender and secretive as a child's his touch lingered, arrested by a pulse kicking madly against his exploring fingers. Catriona jerked up her head and in the space of a gasp their glances met . . . and clung . . . and began tentatively probing.

It seemed at that moment, while she stood locked in his tight embrace, hypnotised by a glittering, amber-flecked stare accustomed to exploring the sexual jungle, to sizing up, selecting and tracking down a mate, that the entire world sighed to a standstill—wind abating to a soft breeze; heaving sea

to a gently rocking cradle, banks of grey cloud part-
ing to make way for sunshine that bathed her frozen
limbs in a molten glow.

'Kate,' he husked, lowering his russet-red head
until his breath was brushing smooth as pelt against
her lips, 'you should always wear your hair down
... I've never seen you looking more attractive,
more excitingly responsive.'

Her soft mouth quivered, then lifted trustingly
towards his, drawn in spite of herself to experience
for a second time a kiss that had reacted upon her
senses like a first sip of champagne, that had made
her head spin, her mouth feel dry, her lips hungry
for the taste of sparkling sweetness.

With the triumph of a thief who has been handed
the key to a guarded vault, Leon plundered with
impunity, kissing her eyes, her cheeks, her ears, then
burying his lips in the velvet softness of her neck
until she was quivering with sensations she could
neither control nor understand but which she instinctively knew had been taught by Adam to his
newly-created Eve. Nothing seemed to exist except
his fiercely demanding lips and the sound of two
hearts pounding as one. But when his hands began
fumbling beneath her sweater, shock jolted through
her ingenuous body so that she stiffened suddenly,
then caught him unawares by clawing like a wildcat
out of his lusty embrace.

From a yard away she directed a glare that was a
combination of self-contempt and disgust of his
audacious trespass.

'What do you think you're doing?' she stormed.
'What sort of girl do you think I am?'

For a second he appeared stunned, then he gathered himself together to complete her mortification with a slight shrug of amusement.

'Responding as any man would to signals set at green, is the answer to your first question,' he drawled. 'But as for your second—well, I haven't quite made up my mind. Only a flirtatious tease or a naïve fool would follow up a come-on with an instant freeze, so I'll decide later when I've had more opportunity to further our acquaintance.'

This reminder that she had met him more than halfway, that some sort of brainstorm had egged her into displaying an eagerness for his advances she could neither explain nor understand, sent colour flaring into her cheeks. Suddenly the need to erect a barrier became imperative, an armour of indifference behind which she could hide her desperate vulnerability.

'What a typically male reaction!' She managed to imitate a trill of scornful laughter. 'Thousands of years ago when we lived in caves and wore animal skins, men were expected to be wild and women to be tame, to respond meekly to man's roving eye, his quick arousal, his desire for a one-night stand without any kind of serious commitment. But in today's society—as I've had cause to point out previously—women demand equal status with men, have fought for the freedom to choose for themselves not only their career but also with whom they go to bed! I'm not surprised that you're still a bachelor,' she forced a final mocking insult, 'obviously, you have yet to learn that much ground is lost by men being too quick too soon! Modern girls prefer subtlety to domination, expect to be given time to decide whether to commit themselves to a flame that devours or to the steady warmth of a fire less easily extinguished.'

It did much for her ego to see the caveman who flaunted his superiority so nonplussed. Her elation was such that she did not flinch even when he made a swift recovery and snarled,

'Feminist is merely another word for a frustrated freak who wants to have her cake and eat it too! If the day should ever dawn when I'm reduced to allowing a woman to buy me a drink or a meal, or to giving her time to consider whether or not she wants me to make love to her, I'll retreat to a monastery! Grab yourself a notebook and pencil, Miss Dunross,' he snapped, seething with frustration. 'Having a dolly bird secretary could have been fun, but as you're obviously averse to filling such a role, I aim to make certain that you slave hard as any roughneck for every dollar you earn!'

CHAPTER SEVEN

The tip of Catriona's pencil fairly flew across the page of her notebook as she raced to transcribe the minutes of a meeting called by Leon to instruct departmental heads upon the edict from head office, to test their reactions and to invite their comments. For almost an hour he had talked non-stop and at a speed guaranteed to strain the ability of the most expert shorthand writer, but in spite of his use of unfamiliar words and technical jargon that dripped smooth as black gold from oil men's lips, she was enjoying the challenge, elated by the assurance that in one area at least she could hold her own with the man who used words instead of thumbscrews, who had stretched her endurance to the limit on a rack of emotion.

Yet as the meeting proceeded she was forced to acknowledge his superb handling of irate men whose stubborn opposition to his arguments was tempered with respect and the friendly rapport that enabled him to be on first name terms with every employee from the senior administrator to the youngest galley boy.

'Look here, Leon,' the young toolpusher who was head of the drilling team jumped angrily to his feet, 'it's all very well for bosses sitting in comfortable offices to pontificate about making economies, but if they were brought out here to have their memories refreshed about the conditions in which my men work they'd sing a very different tune! Which has priority, the saving of a few dollars or the safety of drilling crews who have the vitally important job of keeping the well under control at all times in case gas seeping up the hole should cause a blow-out?'

'Everybody's job is important on board an oil rig,' a grim-looking production supervisor reminded him. 'Your guys may get the oil out, but mine have the equally demanding job of ensuring that it's pumped safely to the mainland.'

Fiercely the young toolpusher retaliated. 'They don't work covered from head to foot in mud, with soaking wet feet and——'

'Nor do they have to clean up after themselves!' A third voice joined in the argument. 'Considering the fact that bedlinen is changed every day, fresh towels are supplied, filthy boiler suits are washed and personal items of clothing laundered, a ratio of four stewards to almost two hundred other workers can hardly be considered excessive. Don't you agree, Leon?'

Suddenly another voice exploded, 'What a load of——'

Catriona kept her lashes demurely downcast as if revising the contents of her writing pad, so as to alleviate the embarrassment of the catering manager, whose explosive outburst had been cut short by a sudden reminder of her presence. She had to struggle to suppress a smile when, choking back his imprecation, he continued with mild heat,

'If you want to see men working then come and cast your eyes over my galley slaves, the catering staff without whom this rig would cease being operational within twenty-four hours! Working in a region that's fit for only fish and seagulls, meals become the highlight of every man's day. My staff has to provide round the clock service, often serving breakfasts and dinners to men sharing the same table, with food as good as any provided by a first class hotel!'

'Gentlemen, please!' With his usual economy of words Leon stepped in to referee the verbal punch-up. 'Don't let's waste time arguing about who contributes most to the running of the platform. I don't need to be told that every man aboard is here because his skills are essential to our operation, nor do I need reassurance from experts in charge, who've learned their jobs on oil installations all over the world, all I ask is that you try to see the situation from my point of view. As Director of Operations, I have the job of communicating to you all directives received from head office and doing my best to ensure that they're implemented. Perhaps I've been wrong,' even Catriona was affected by the despondency of his shrug, 'but in the past I've always prided myself upon the fact that we work, not as individuals in search of personal glory, but as a team whose main aim has always been to maintain production and at the same time ensure the safety and welfare of the men aboard this rig. Never be in any doubt that the aim remains the same! Economies have been *asked* for—not demanded—because of a worldwide depression that has turned the commercial marketplace into an arena of cut-throat competition, but it has to be you, the experts in charge, who make the relevant decisions! Without your co-operation my task will be made ten times more difficult. Am I asking too much of you guys . . .?'

Catriona wanted to jump to her feet and applaud the cleverly-calculated, beautifully-delivered performance that had raised the oil men's pride yet at the same time had managed to reduce tough, belligerent individuals to the level of schoolboy miscreants shifting uncomfortably in their seats. Undoubtedly, she excused her own lapse of will power, her rugged boss possessed a magnetism that made him a danger to opponents of either sex.

'I suppose,' the gruff production supervisor was the first to respond to Leon's appeal, 'I could take a second look at my figures.'

'And I might start laying down the law to gluttons who consider six T-bone steaks a normal meal,' the catering manager grudgingly conceded.

'You can count on all of us, Leon,' the young toolpusher spoke up for the rest of them, 'we'll do everything we can to help.'

'Thank you, men.' When Leon's mouth relaxed into a smile of appreciation Catriona noticed indications of strain that must have been building up inside him during the past hectic weeks. For the very first time his amber eyes lacked the sparkle of a lion on the chase; his voice had grown gruff with over-use, and when he sat back in his chair to flex tired shoulder muscles she was reminded of a strong beast too long overburdened.

'Catriona!' She swung round startled and blushed when Geoff Barclay's teasing grin communicated his awareness of her close scrutiny of her boss. 'I've had a washroom set aside for your personal use for the duration of your stay on the rig. Being a family man myself, with a couple of daughters, I know how upset girls can become if they're deprived too long of the chance to pretty themselves up.'

Because of the length of time they had spent travelling, tramping around the rig, and the couple of hours she had spent working in an atmosphere thick with the eye-smarting smoke of tobacco, her choice of ultimate luxury at that moment would have been soap, hot water, and clean, soft towels.

'Thank you, Geoff, for being so understanding.' Swiftly, she gathered up her belongings and followed him out of the room full of men still engrossed in conversation. 'I hope your womenfolk appreciate your good qualities as much as I do,' she addressed her remarks to broad shoulders leading the way down a narrow alleyway. 'Most men, our boss included, strike me as being single-minded experts at protecting their own interests.'

'Don't blame Leon too much,' he tossed across his shoulder, 'he's had more opportunity than most to practise self-preservation.'

'You've known each other a long time, then?' she queried, alerted by a previously unnoticed trace of transatlantic accent.

'Since boyhood,' he nodded. 'We played together as children in a small oil town that seemed to have a rig on every street corner. Like many others, we worked our way through college by roustabouting and roughnecking on the land rigs. Our training was done in the field, working around the mud pits, before we qualified as engineers and began working for whichever oil patch offered the best prospects—whether in frozen Alaska, the sweltering Gulf States, or the inhospitable North Sea. But whereas most of the time I've been lucky enough to keep my family with me, Leon has no close relatives. He lost both parents when he was around eight years old and the aunt who brought him up—although she must have had some good in her to take him in the first place—was kept too busy holding the interest of a succession of boy-friends to have much time to spare for Leon.'

She heard his deep, throaty chuckle. 'He was a regular Huckleberry Finn in those days, a red-haired, freckled, barefooted urchin who never went hungry simply because there wasn't a woman in town whose heart-strings weren't plucked by his look of pathos as he hung around their porches at meal-times.' When he halted suddenly and turned round to face her she was surprised by his sombre, worried expression.

'Leon hasn't changed much in that respect, Catriona, the woman hasn't been born yet that he can't twist around his little finger. But, probably because of the emotional thrashings he received as a youngster, his attitude towards the opposite sex has always seemed tinged with distrust, as if he suspects that, just like his aunt, all females are too shallow and fickle in nature to remain faithful to any one man.'

Sensing that she was expected to show some sign of shock, or at the very least indignation, Catriona searched for words to convey the suitable reaction of a loving fiancée but managed only one stilted word.

'Really?'

To her relief he seemed too concerned to notice her brevity. Brooding deeply, he nodded, then continued outlining his theory. 'Leon's deep-rooted cynicism was illustrated by an incident that occurred some years ago when we were both members of a team of divers employed to explore the possibilities of a stretch of water off the coast of Australia. Sharks, curious, unpredictable creatures that pose the greatest threat to divers, were abundant. One female in particular seemed to form an attachment to Leon. Each time he dived she would appear, then begin lazily circling, encroaching closer and closer, her rows of wicked teeth bared in the semblance of a smile; narrow eyes glinting, and with huge fins that brushed past Leon with a gesture that was almost flirtatious. He grew very fond of that shark and in spite of our warnings he allowed the caprice to escalate to the stage where he was permitted, even encouraged, to reach out a hand to tickle the underside of her belly as she glided slowly past him. Then,' he sighed, 'the inevitable happened. Without rhyme or reason, she attacked. Fortunately, Leon didn't lose his head but reacted swiftly by repelling her with a heavy blow on the end of her nose, then, instead of trying to make his escape, he swam straight towards her—a shock tactic that resulted in the shark turning tail to swim away, never to be seen again. Ironically, he christened that maneater Mary Lou, after his aunt,' he concluded heavily, 'and to my certain knowledge she was the last female ever to persuade Leon to relax his guard.'

He smiled down at Catriona's startled face.

'Perhaps now you'll forgive my ill-mannered show of surprise when you were introduced as his fiancée? Leon needs someone like you, Catriona, a girl who'll give him what he swears he doesn't want but which every other man takes for granted—a stable home life, tender loving care, and later on perhaps, when he's ready for it, the most priceless gift of all, the replica of himself that's handed to a guy all pretty and pink and giftwrapped in a dainty baby shawl!'

As Geoff was so obviously delighted by the prospect of seeing his friend settling down at last, she had no heart to disabuse him, but as she indulged in a refreshing wash and ran the comb he had so thoughtfully provided through wind-tangled tresses her conscience rebelled against the need to continue a deception she had been driven into by necessity and which, because it suited his purpose, Leon was constructing into a web of deceit inside which she felt trapped by the knowledge that any attempt to escape would result in the immediate destruction of her aunt's new-found happiness.

Reluctantly, when she felt she could dally no longer, she made her way back to the office where the meeting had been held and felt speared by an accusing glare immediately she stepped over the threshold.

'Where the blazes have you been?' Leon growled, pausing his prowl of the empty room as soon as she appeared.

'Enjoying a wash and brush-up,' she countered, mustering spirit in order to conceal her nervousness. 'There's nothing in my contract that states I have to be at your beck and call twenty-four hours a day!'

'And do you feel better for it?' His tone, implying that no improvement was obvious, spilled acid on to her already smarting pride.

'I'm aware that I look a sight,' she snapped, hating his slow, amused perusal of a shirt shrunk by many washings, tightly confining thrusting breasts with the aid of one tiny mother-of-pearl button upon which modesty was imposing an impossible strain, and upon the flowing line of thigh and rounded buttocks that looked poured into a skin of faded denim. 'I suspect that you deliberately set out to embarrass me by leaving me no time to change!'

'Into one of the demure-nun outfits you've taken to wearing in the office? Not likely! It was quite a revelation seeing you dressed as a saucy little tart, amply confirming my theory that your aim was to titillate my curiosity. I much prefer your honest, trash-with-flash image.'

'*Trash with flash!*' she gasped, casting a horrified glance at the cast-offs that had drawn not the slightest hint of criticism from her spinster aunt. 'How dare you!' she choked. 'You know perfectly well that when you arrived at the cottage I was ready to begin decorating!'

'So you were,' he agreed, displaying the cynicism of a man wary of being twice bitten, 'and because I wasn't expected, you dressed to complement your flirtatious nature. In future, please don't bother wrapping up in pretence for my benefit, I much prefer stark naked reality!'

'I'll bear that in mind,' she spat, incensed by his laboured insistence that she had set out deliberately to capture his attention. 'Such knowledge might just come in useful if ever I'm foolish enough to allow your preferences to assume one iota of importance to me! Meanwhile,' she rushed on, unbearably goaded, 'perhaps you'll begin revising your opinion that all women are fashioned in the same image as your aunt. I for one am no *femme fatale* hungry for masculine attention!'

'Who told you about my aunt?' His cold, emotionless tone was more deadly than temper. 'On second thoughts, I hardly need ask. Geoff's continuous residence in a household full of women is turning him into an inveterate gossip!'

'Please, Leon, don't be angry with him!' Her remorse ran so deep that in her agitation she was not conscious of using his christian name. 'Geoff did explain a little of your background, but only because he felt it might help me to understand you better—and then only because he'd been given the impression that you and I are more than just good friends. You must be aware,' she urged desperately, alarmed by lines of displeasure tightening his features into a mask of cold disdain, 'how horrified he'd be if ever he were to be charged with breaking the confidence of a friend. All he wanted was to enlist my sympathy—he certainly had no idea that he was delivering a weapon into the hands of an enemy!'

'Is that how you see us, Kate?' His lips twisted. 'As sworn enemies locked in conflict?'

As the question hung in the air between them she hesitated, undecided whether his change of tactics was just another trick, or if his lack of fire was a genuine reaction to the weeks of strain and overwork that had upset her own equilibrium. Weary or not, the king of beasts was not to be trusted. Yet when he shifted sideways into a patch of shadow that darkened the hollows beneath high cheekbones and doused every glint in his fiery hair, she was swamped by an urge to give him the benefit of the doubt.

'Aunt Hanna has often accused me of perversity,' she almost apologised in a tone so muted he was forced to step nearer in order to catch the trembling words. 'From our first moment of meeting I've felt some dark spirit of recalcitrance pulling me in a direction I hadn't intended to go. I can't lay claim to a previously angelic disposition,' heavy lashes lifted to direct a pleading look from green eyes dark with puzzlement, 'but neither can I remember ever being so beastly to any person other than yourself.'

It was his turn to look surprised, to scour her face with the narrow-eyed, watchful stare of an animal with hackles half risen. A blush of mortification seeped slowly into her cheeks while she waited with eyes downcast, wrestling with the knowledge that her foolish, trusting heart had delivered her into the hands of an unscrupulous adversary.

However, Leon's response, though slow in coming, held no trace of derision but was more a hesitant, over-cautious acceptance of her olive branch.

'Strange that you should say that,' he admitted, sounding as if his vocal chords were being jerked by clumsy fingers. 'My reputation for being beastly is well known, yet there have been times,' he paused, then forced the surprising confession, 'especially during the past weeks, when your aptitude for hard work and willing co-operation have lulled me into a mood saintly enough to rout the devil!'

'Oh . . .!' Her head lifted to reveal a face startled as a round-mouthed child's—and as diffidently uncertain how to cope.

Predictably, Leon took charge, rescuing her from the morass of confusion into which she had been plunged by proffering an invitation in a voice holding more than a hint of amused transatlantic drawl.

'Suddenly I feel hungry. Would you care to celebrate our armistice by joining me for a meal?'

Her spirits rocketed, enabling her to tease with sparkling eyes. 'Only if I'm to be allowed a free choice of menu. I remember reading somewhere that Americans can eat garbage provided it's liberally sprinkled with ketchup, mustard, chilli sauce, tabasco sauce, cayenne pepper, or any other condiment that destroys the original flavour of the dish!'

The dining-room was filled with chatter and happy smiling faces, all of which swivelled in their direction immediately they walked through the doorway. Then to Catriona's utter confusion a roar of cheering and shouts of congratulation accompanied their progress towards a table that had obviously been graced in readiness for their arrival with a spotless white cloth, sparkling cutlery and a hastily constructed cardboard banner scrawled with the word 'Congratulations' hanging from a lamp positioned directly overhead.

Blushing with embarrassment, reluctant to meet Leon's eyes, she murmured a few words of appreciation to the hovering catering manager, managed a wave of acknowledgment to the grinning men, then dived for cover behind a typewritten menu.

'Such a shame we can't run to a bottle of champagne,' the manager sighed, 'but unfortunately alcohol is forbidden aboard the platform. However,' he brightened, 'for starters I can offer a choice of prawn cocktail, cream of tomato soup or fresh salmon Hollandaise. For the main course you can choose from baked York ham with pineapple, fillet of beef Wellington or a cold buffet. Then if you should care for dessert, I can personally recommend the sherry trifle, although Leon, I know, prefers to round off his meal with cheese and biscuits.'

'Just a little soup and a small helping of salad will do fine, thank you,' Catriona decided, chancing an upward glance before daring to remind Leon, 'You told Aunt Hanna to expect us back for dinner. She's sure to have prepared a substantial meal.'

'I hadn't forgotten.' His easy smile sent butterflies stampeding through her stomach. 'However, as it's just midday, I intend appeasing my Yankee appetite with the fillet of beef. Can't I persuade you to abandon your choice of rabbit food in favour of something more substantial?'

'No, thank you,' she could not resist the tease, 'my choice seems most applicable, considering the fact that the rabbit is often classed as a domestic pet one of those unfortunates provided by Nature to be kicked whenever things go wrong within its immediate circle.'

'In that case I'm pleased I offered to feed you,' he retaliated with a wicked glint, 'for pets are purported always to remember the crumbs they are tossed, but to forget every stone that's ever been thrown at their heads.'

CHAPTER EIGHT

GOOD humour spiced each course of a meal that became pleasantly extended as they conversed freely and easily for the very first time. The scraping of chairs across a tiled floor, the jocular greetings and farewells being exchanged by the occupants of surrounding tables as they to-ed and fro-ed between changing shifts, barely impinged upon their absorption as they probed and delved, discovering many areas of previously unexplored agreement.

Occasionally Catriona glanced up, distracted by a freshening draught slamming doors into their frames, rattling windows, swirling menus and paper napkins cleanly from tables to begin a mischievous paperchase across the width of the floor. But as Leon appeared unconcerned about what might have been the build-up to a storm, she did not dwell upon the implications but relaxed, contenting herself with the mild observation,

'A storm seems to be brewing.'

'No need to feel nervous,' he smiled, stirring a liberal helping of sugar into his coffee. 'The platform may look like a bit of Meccano sticking out of the sea, but it's been designed and built to withstand winds gusting at a hundred and sixty miles per hour and waves the height of a ten-storey building.'

'Are you overlooking the fact that I've lived most of my life on an island swept with wind and gales, kept isolated during most of the winter months by terrible waters?' she reminded, amused by the notion that he should think her fearful. 'Some say we Shelties are born wearing a bobble cap and wellies!'

'And yet you're all very partisan on the subject of your island and very loath to leave it,' he puzzled curiously. 'I must confess I can't understand why, when there are so many less isolated and far more hospitable places to live than Shetland. It's always been my theory that isolated places breed solitary people.'

'I've often felt lonelier in a crowd of faceless people than I've felt tramping the hills of home,' she confessed simply. 'Whenever I talk to the ponies and sheep they at least respond with genuine feeling, not with social chit-chat meaningless as tinkling cymbals.'

Unaware of his surprised attention, of amber-bright eyes staring keenly, she continued dreamily, 'Real conversation is the constant flow of charming speech exchanged by old women wearing shawls and leather knitting belts whose wit matches the flashing steel of needles converting wool into exquisite garments that have intricate patterns unique to the knitter's mind. Or the leisurely, almost grudging sparsity of words bartered by old fishermen whose calloused hands have steered boats through terrible gales and pitiless rain, striving against unimaginable odds, in order to net the fish essential to their families' survival. I'm quite certain,' she lifted a flushed, earnest face to plead, 'that if you should really set out to get to know our island well, you would begin to appreciate it almost as much as I do. You've judged it from afar, Leon, hardly setting foot outside of your huge man-made complex that's as alien to Shetland as a strange new planet. But if you could leave your car behind and walk with me on foot I could show you charming old crofts with roofs lowering over tiny windows crammed with mint, thyme and sweet-smelling sage, built so close to the shore their doorsteps are stained white, cured by the constant washing of salted sea-foam. I could show you hills massed with tiny flowers blazoning every colour of the rainbow; voes thrusting arrow-straight through jagged cliffs; take you to see otters at play and to where ponies graze and peer indignantly through a fringe of shaggy hair at whoever dares to interrupt their meal.'

She broke off, suddenly becoming conscious of his stare, X-ray-deep, probing for hidden motives. Shocked by the realisation that her runaway tongue had caused enthusiasm to sound like eager invitation, she blushed and hastened to make light of her embarrassing gaffe.

'I'm sorry, I must have sounded just then like the islands' public relations officer!'

'By definition,' his transatlantic drawl was clearly evident, 'a public relations exercise is a deliberate, planned, and sustained effort to establish and maintain mutual understanding between an organisation and its public. Speaking on behalf of the organisation,' he pinned her with a narrow-eyed look, 'I shall be glad to take you up on your offer of a tour of the island at the first available opportunity. You're quite right in your condemnation; I've rarely strayed far from the camp and consequently know little about the island or its inhabitants.'

Because she felt stalked, alarmed by the dangerous soft-padded approach of a well-fed lion in search in female diversion, Catriona panicked and began a babbling attempt to channel his thoughts towards a safer subject of conversation.

'Sandra mentioned that her boy-friend Gordon works here on the rig,' she dodged with breathless haste. 'I'd very much like to meet him.'

'I'm sorry,' he drawled, obviously amused by his quarry's swift change of direction, 'that simply isn't possible.'

'Why not?' she persisted, doggedly determined to stay one step ahead. 'I know he's here at present, Sandra told me so.'

'Quite rightly,' he nodded. 'The fact that he's doing a spell of duty is the reason why you can't meet him.'

'I don't understand . . .'

With a resigned shrug, Leon abandoned further baiting and took pity on her bewilderment. 'Deep sea diving is a complex and extremely dangerous job—one very experienced diver was killed when simply testing equipment in a few feet of water. Gordon is what's known as a saturation diver, one who spends his time working from a tiny diving bell positioned on the sea-bed, and between shifts he, and the rest of his team, live like monks in metal cells, deprived of all luxuries, denied even cigarettes, inside a small decompression chamber on a support vessel anchored nearby.'

Wide-eyed with wonder, she stammered, 'But that's appalling! Surely men who are forced to live in such conditions must suffer marked ill effects?'

Frowning, he shook his head. 'Periodically, each

diver receives a medical check-up to ensure that his physical condition hasn't deteriorated.'

'But they must be subjected to terrific mental strain,' she protested. 'Medical examinations can ascertain any change in glandular function, blood pressure, pulse and respiration rates, but can give no indication of the state of a person's emotions!'

She had not intended to sound condemnatory, but her sharp tone must have pricked some tender area of conscience, causing his frown to deepen.

'Diving is a self-selecting business,' he defended sharply. 'It's extraordinary how quickly the weak are weeded out until only stable, courageous, wholly dedicated characters remain.'

'And yet,' she countered, treading warily as a tenderfoot over thorns, 'divers have the reputation of taking suicidal risks on shore when driving cars or motor-cycles—surely an indication of mental instability?'

'Nonsense,' he denied crisply, aggravation rippling his smooth pelt of certitude. 'Would you judge a man insane simply because, after weeks of courting danger, he lets off steam by living life to the full? I know my men, understand what makes them tick, because I've shared with them the new and terrifying hazards facing divers working at deeper and deeper levels where any sudden, drastic change in pressure might explode the fillings in a man's teeth or reduce his body to a mass of quivering jelly! I've known the rigours of working from a small steel ball lowered on to the sea-bed, have suffered the freezing cold and the narcotic effect of breathing nitrogen under pressure which produces a sensation divers call "rapture of the deep" during which time divers have been known to tear off their face masks in a mood of gay abandon. Consequently,' he concluded grimly, 'I can't condemn them for seizing every opportunity to let off steam with riotous living.'

'But why do they choose to do such a job?' she persisted shaken by his lurid description. 'What motivates men to endure the extremes of dicing with death and then languishing for long boring hours inside a decompression chamber with less comfort than a prison cell? It can't just be the thought of money piling up in their bank accounts!'

His musing half-smile, the secretive, faraway look in his eyes, erected a barrier beyond which she sensed no one other than a member of the exclusive, tightly-knit diving fraternity could ever hope to penetrate.

'Divers are undoubtedly a mercenary crowd of individuals,' he admitted finally. 'Because of the risks they take and the fact that they live like nomads, their attitude has to be to get as much money as possible while they can, for once their diving career is over, or they become unfit for diving, they know they'll have great difficulty settling down to an ordinary job that pays very ordinary money. Yet having said that,' he confided with a complacency that set her teeth on edge, 'I must admit that men who choose to become divers, though not indifferent to wealth, place it low on their list of priorities. They're mostly what one might term "buccaneering types", men who, had they been born earlier, might have served on ships flying the skull and crossbones simply because they'd discovered that there's more money to be made at sea than on land; adventurers, dedicated to the search for treasure, yet prepared to abide by the rule of "no prey, no pay" if ever there's no loot to be shared.'

Catriona blinked, dazed by the image his words had conjured, an image of a rig topped by a pirate flag, commanded by a red-haired, fiery-tempered captain who restrained his motley crew with the threat of forty lashes!

Making a determined effort to dismiss the fanciful notion, she glanced at her wristwatch and was amazed to discover how quickly the hours had flown while they had been absorbed in conversation.

'Good heavens, it can't be three o'clock already!' She risked an upward glance, almost prepared to see him sporting a piratical eye patch or a large golden earring, and discovered to her relief that he looked his normal mocking self. 'If your business has been concluded, shouldn't we be setting off for the mainland?'

'Didn't I tell you?' His casual tone was belied by a glint of enjoyment in amused amber eyes. 'While the meeting was still in progress the radio operator received a message warning that, as the airfield in Shetland is fogbound, all aircraft have been grounded.'

'You mean we're stranded out here?' In spite of her effort to appear calm Catriona could not conceal a rising note of anxiety.

Predictably, Leon took advantage of her show of weakness. 'Does it matter?' he pounced. 'When I warned you about just such an eventuality, didn't you refuse to acknowledge it as an insuperable problem and argue that if the situation should ever arise you would prefer me to disregard the fact that you're a member of the opposite sex and to treat you as I would treat another man?'

She swallowed hard then, biting back the admission that her request had been voiced before she had plumbed the depths of his character, before she had a chance to realise that there was no place for a woman aboard an ocean rig which, just as in pirate ships of long ago, was crewed by men who regarded females merely as objects to amuse, or to satiate lust. It took all her courage to outstare the man whom bitter lessons from the past had made dangerously unpredictable, a man wary, however much tempted, of being weaned away from the belief that all women were as fickle and uncaring as the aunt whose indifference had turned a trusting boy into an embittered man.

'Personally, I couldn't care less,' she lied, managing what she hoped would appear to be an indifferent shrug, 'but Aunt Hanna is bound to start worrying when I don't turn up for dinner.'

'I've already taken care of that problem,' he smiled, relaxing in his chair with a complacent ease that gave rise to the suspicion that the whole situation had been foreseen—*possibly contrived*! '. . . a radio message has been sent to base, explaining our position and instructing that a messenger should relay the information to your aunt immediately.'

Struggling to subdue newly-born suspicions, she watched him indolently flexing his muscles before rising to his feet. 'Being stranded is no excuse for wasting time,' he grinned cheerfully. 'While I begin an in-depth tour of operations, perhaps you would

like to start typing out the minutes of the meeting—
I've told Geoff to supply you with a desk and typewriter. See you later,' he concluded with infuriating
aplomb, then, pretending not to notice her scandalised expression, began leisurely strolling away.

Immediately Geoff arrived to escort her to a small
office just big enough to accommodate a desk, a chair
and one slim-line filing cabinet she sensed an indefinable change in his attitude.

'If there's anything else you need don't hesitate to
ask, my office is just along the passageway,' he told
her in a tone that sounded friendly, yet reserved.
Telling herself that she had no right to feel hurt
merely because his heartwarming grin was missing,
because the fatherly concern he had displayed towards her from the moment they had been introduced had disappeared, to be replaced by the look
of a man who felt let down, somehow disappointed,
she smiled back warmly, consoling herself with the
reassurance that a man with such a responsible job
could be forgiven an occasional air of distraction.

'Thank you, Geoff—but as usual, you seem to
have provided everything I'm likely to need.
Although why I should be expected to work on my
day off, especially when this typing could quite easily
have waited until Monday, I can't imagine,' she
concluded on a note of asperity.

'The pattern of Leon's life has long been estab-
lished as being one of work, sleep, and eat, in that
order—with the exception, of course, of minor
diversions,' he responded dryly.

For some curious reason she felt scolded as a
schoolgirl caught scrumping apples and in spite of

the fact that she had filched nothing, had broken no known rules, a blush of guilt fired her cheeks as she turned aside, pretending an interest in the contents of the office. Then, still smarting from the suspicion that she had lapsed from favour, she blurted impulsively when Geoff turned to leave,

'Although I'm quite used to the vagaries of local weather, I find it puzzling that, with such strong winds blowing around the platform, the reason given for our delayed flight is that the airport is fogbound. Surely wind and fog are two contradictory elements?'

When Geoff spun on his heel with a quizzical look she felt a twinge of shame for suspecting Leon's motives, and was even more ashamed when he confirmed the truth of the statement.

'You must remember that there are almost two hundred miles of sea separating us and the islands. It's quite usual, even in summer, for the platform to be clear while the whole of Shetland is fogbound. Often flights are delayed for a day or more, other times we're lucky and the fog clears up quicker than expected.'

'Oh, I'm glad to hear it,' she mumbled, then, seeking to excuse her unworthy suspicions she stammered, 'It's . . . it's just that I don't want my aunt to think that . . . er . . .'

'I understand,' he cut in abruptly, this time making no secret of his cold disapproval. 'I think what you're trying to say is that sometimes a bad excuse is worse than no excuse at all.'

For the following four hours Catriona pounded away at her typewriter, hampered by the fact that all her fingers seemed to have turned into thumbs; that the strange machine had odd keys in positions unfamiliar to her, and by anger that had erupted the moment she spotted the note Leon had placed upon her desk, informing her that he required one copy of the minutes to be handed to each of the departmental heads before they left the platform the following morning. Furiously, she worked, hitting wrong keys and correcting many mistakes, cursing the inconsideration of a boss who seemed to find pleasure in overloading her with work, who must have been aware that with the aid of equipment back at base she would have needed to type out only one set of minutes before obtaining the rest of the number required with the help of a photostat copying machine. But her main drawback to concentration was worry about Geoff's change of attitude, a worry that did not ease until backbreaking hours later, when after slinging the cover over her typewriter and clipping foolscap pages neatly in order, she set out in search of him, determined to clear the air with a confrontation.

She found him alone in his office, but immediately she stepped inside he took the wind completely out of her sails with an astonishing greeting.

'Ah, Catriona! I'm pleased you've finished your work in time for me to show you to your cabin before I make my way to the mess hall for dinner. Leon's busy at the moment,' he told her, his expression wooden, 'but he's asked me to pass on the message that you're to choose whichever bunk you find most comfortable as he can sleep equally well in the upper or lower berth.'

If a clenched fist had landed against her solar plexus she could not have been more winded. Embarrassment ran molten hot through her veins as she stared at Geoff, every puzzling question answered by his obvious effort to maintain an expression of studied indifference. Her lips parted to utter an immediate protest, to state plainly and unequivocally that she had no intention of sharing a cabin with any man, much less her boss-cum-temporary fiancé, but even as the first hot word scorched the tip of her tongue realisation struck, fusing her lips into silence.

Her refusal to accept conditions aboard the platform was the whole object of Leon's exercise! The tool with which he hoped to prise her out of her job without fear of any backlash from head office, or the inconvenience of having to spare time for the legal formalities that were bound to follow hard on the heels of any protest she might make to the appropriate authorities on the grounds of unfair dismissal.

> '*Yond Cassius has a lean and hungry look:*
> *He thinks too much: such men are dangerous.*'

How aptly the quotation fitted the lean, revenge-hungry boss of Lion Oil Incorporated!

Feeling lightheaded as a climber saved by pure instinct from falling into a hidden abyss, Catriona expelled a shuddering breath and took a second or · two to quell her rioting senses.

'Thank you, Geoff, I'll be glad to retire to my cabin. As I'm feeling very tired and not at all hungry, would you mind conveying my excuses for not turning up for dinner?'

Although to her own ears, her emotionless words had sounded very far off, their effect upon Geoff was dramatic. 'Look here, Catriona,' he glared, striding round his desk towards her, 'I can't go along with this farce a moment longer! I know Leon is capable of holding you to your word, of forcing you to endure the limitations of a male-orientated society, but I refuse to believe you're the very liberated lady you're pretending to be. On the contrary,' he snorted angrily, 'just like my wilful, bra-waving daughters, you're hiding behind a front of bravado! Let me tell Leon, on your behalf, to go to hell, Catriona,' he urged. 'I can't think of any errand that would give me greater pleasure!'

Consoled by his bluff show of concern, she wavered, but when an image of her aunt's wrinkled face flashed into her mind's eye she squared her shoulders.

'Thank you for feeling concerned about me, Geoff, but there's a very good reason why the situation must be allowed to stand,' she declined gently. 'Please don't interfere, I know that basically you and Leon share a very deep bond—I should hate to be the cause of a rift between such good friends.'

To her relief Geoff accepted her decision without further argument. After guiding her wordlessly through a labyrinth of passageways he stopped eventually outside the door of a cabin situated as far away as possible from the noise of heavy machinery penetrating even to the heart of the platform as a low, vibrating grumbling.

'This is Leon's cabin, earmarked for his own personal use,' he informed her gruffly, swinging the unlocked door wide. 'I'm sorry I can't offer you a key—there are two, but Leon has them both. However, you'll find my number on the pad next to the telephone. If you want me for any reason don't hesitate to dial.'

When he left her inside a spartan room just large enough to accommodate two bunks, an easy chair, a small table, and a wardrobe fitted into a narrow recess, the headache that had begun as a niggle while she was typing accelerated into a dull, throbbing ache against her temples. Wearily she dropped on to the lower bunk and stretched supine, intending to remain there just long enough for her headache to subside. But as she listened to the dull throbbing that reverberated twenty-four hours a day throughout the platform her eyelids grew heavier and heavier until finally all sounds faded.

'Kate, wake up!'

When the imperious command penetrated her slumber she opened her eyes and twisted round to stare dazedly at an unfamiliar lamp; cream-painted walls, strangely-patterned curtains and bedspread. Then when a patch of shadow moved she jerked upright to stare with startled green eyes into the smiling face of the company boss. The rude awakening could not have left her more unprepared, less able to cope with a traumatic, potentially dangerous situation.

He was sitting on the side of her bunk, leaning so close she could have stretched out a hand and traced every line of mocking humour playing around his lips. Given no time to gather her scattered thoughts, she betrayed her vulnerability with a rush of hot, fiery colour.

'Why the guilty blush, Kate?' he murmured, stroking a possessive hand along the curve of her cheek. 'True innocence is ashamed of nothing.'

She stiffened with alarm when, deliberately audacious, he slid a stroking caress along her slender neck, down past her shirt collar, then began exploring the hidden silkiness of her shoulder. Numbed with shock, she tried to jerk away, but was trapped when he began exerting pressure upon her shoulder, pressing her back against the pillows. Then deliberately, and with a coolness that increased her shame, he plucked free the small, strategically placed button holding together both edges of the shirt strained tightly across her breasts.

'I've waited all day for that damned button to pop,' he confessed with a low growl of laughter, casting an amber-bright gaze of appreciation over exposed curves pulsating madly, gleaming pale and tender as innocence.

'Have you gone completely mad?' she croaked through a throat tight with fear when his head, with its mane of burnished hair, began lowering purposefully towards her. He hesitated, his lips twisted cynically.

'Aren't I reacting exactly as you expected— exactly as you *planned*!' he smouldered. 'I never withhold praise that's due; you planned your campaign like a general, Kate, one possessing a thorough grasp of psychology, the knowledge of how a show of indifference, a slow advance followed by a quick retreat can confuse the enemy. But I think I've cracked the code,' he smiled coldly. 'First comes the freeze, then the slow thaw, next the blatant come-on, and the quick retreat before the cycle begins all over again. According to my reckoning we ought by now to have reached the most interesting stage of your strategy.'

Giving her no time to gasp an amazed denial, his lips swooped down upon hers, thirsty as a traveller in the desert; ravenous as a prisoner denied food, lustful as any virile buccaneer kept too long at sea, too long deprived of feminine solace.

Using white-hot anger as her main weapon, Catriona fought like a she-cat to escape from blistering kisses that ought to have repelled yet somehow managed to ignite shy, unawakened emotions to a pitch of sensuous arousal.

But determined as the king of beasts famed throughout the jungle for commanding looks, magestic manner, and virile reputation, Leon responded to her puny show of resistance with a throaty purr of pleasure, treating her writhing rejection as part of the mating game, the rolling, clawing, sensuous preliminary practised by nympho females intent upon teasing a mate's heat to fever pitch.

Her protests had been smothered to a despairing sigh, her defiant body caressed into a state of quivering acquiescence when the intense atmosphere filled with the racing throb of hearts beating in unison, heavy with an aura of intense inevitability, was shattered by the shrill demanding summons of the telephone.

Immediately, Leon's sinewed shoulders stiffened

beneath her fretful hands and a savage curse ripped from lips sweetened by a first sip of shy, tentative response. He tried to ignore it, but when the piercing shrill was joined by the far-off wailing of a klaxon he responded by jerking angrily aside to grab the received from its cradle.

'What is it? Didn't you receive instructions that I was not to be disturbed?'

'Yes, Leon,' Geoff's calm response was clearly audible, 'but we're on yellow alert.'

Leon snapped to attention. 'Very well, I'll be with you in a couple of minutes—I'll come straight down to the radio room!'

Catriona could not help wondering whether their passionate interlude had been no more than mere fantasy as she lay in a dishevelled, breathless heap staring at the man who barely cast her a glance as he strode towards the door. However, something about her still, distraught figure must have impinged upon his conscience, for he paused just long enough to toss across his shoulder,

'A yellow alert means that there's something out of line that must be investigated immediately in order to avoid a shutdown. It's probably nothing serious, in which case we'll go over to green status and I'll be back very shortly.'

When the door slammed shut behind him she remained numbly staring, feeling cheapened as a chattel by the man whose flow of passion could be stemmed as quickly and easily as oil gushing from underground wells. Then her tear-filled eyes caught the glint of some small shiny object dangling from a chain attached to the lock.

The keys! Without them Leon could not get back into the cabin!

Uttering a cry of thankfulness, she scrambled from the bunk and ran to lock the door.

CHAPTER NINE

IT was a calm, clear morning with hardly a ripple disturbing the surface of deep green sea nor a breath of wind to spoil the accuracy of gannets practising high dives, lazily wheeling and soaring, yet constantly alert for the flash of a silver fin.

Catriona waved and forced her stiff lips into the semblance of a smile as the helicopter engine roared into deafening life and Geoff's burly figure, braced to withstand the force of a powerful air-stream, began receding, then disappeared completely when the craft soared upwards to attain correct flying altitude. Thankful that the noise of rotor blades made normal conversation impossible, she leant back in her seat, keeping her eyes averted from a profile she knew was etched deep with the displeasure of a male who, because he felt cheated, was not disposed to hide his ill humour.

She had no idea whether he had slept or even where he had spent the night, for, in a cowardly attempt to avoid confrontation until the very last moment, she had skipped breakfast and skulked in her cabin until Geoff's cheery voice had persuaded her to unlock the door.

'I've brought you some sandwiches,' he had grinned as he had stepped across the threshold. 'If memory serves me correctly, you've had nothing to eat since lunchtime yesterday.'

Making no show of reluctance, she had accepted them eagerly.

'Thank you, Geoff.' Quickly she had disposed of the plastic wrapping. 'You're an absolute angel!'

'I almost became one last night,' he had twinkled, watching her munching greedily. 'At least, I was cursed to hell and back by your very irate fiancé.'

'You were? But why?' she had puzzled.

With an expression of bland innocence completely at odds with a twinkle of devilry, Geoff had confessed, 'I'm afraid I jumped the gun rather by setting the platform on yellow alert. The cause of the alarm turned out to be nothing more serious than exhaust fumes in one of the turbines, consequently we were back to green status by the time Leon reached the radio room. Never before have I seen him react so badly to having his rest disturbed,' he had confided with such an air of contrived bewilderment she had realised immediately—as Leon obviously had—that the alarm had been deliberately raised, the entire platform disrupted, solely for her benefit! She had stared, stricken dumb with gratitude, moved almost to tears by the first fatherly act of concern she had ever experienced, then because words would have been inadequate she had surprised him by flinging her arms around his neck and standing on tiptoe to express her gratitude with a shy kiss. Unfortunately, Leon had chosen that precise moment to make his appearance!

The flight was accomplished in record time. The moment the craft was grounded she made a hurried descent, then darted across the tarmac intending to make her escape. But after a few yards of freedom she was captured, jolted to a standstill by a painful grip upon her elbow.

'I'll drive you home,' Leon growled, towering vengeful as a predator robbed of his spoils.

'Don't bother,' she declined hastily, trying to shake off his hand. 'I'll walk to the kirk to meet Aunt Hanna, she gets a lift there and back each Sunday morning.'

Ignoring her protest, he guided her towards the car park where his enormous silver-coloured Range Rover—that would have looked more at home transporting parka-clad oilmen across frozen Alaskan wastes—stood glistening in the pale morning sunshine. Not until he had helped her into the passenger seat perched high above the ground did he release his grip upon her elbow in order to swing himself behind the steering wheel and set a mighty lever into first gear. The way in which the car lurched around a corner of the airport building, the deafening roar being forced from an accelerator that needed a mere touch of extra pressure to scale the highest sand dunes, were ample indication of his impatient, savagely resentful mood.

Catriona's fears were proved well founded when after half an hour's driving along the deserted road leading towards her home, he braked and ran the car into a layby poised on top of jagged cliffs, tumbling downward to a narrow, sea-creamed voe.

'Now,' he clenched, engaging the handbrake with a violence that caused her a jolt of alarm, 'would you mind explaining why you locked me out of my cabin last night?'

Urging herself to remain calm in the face of seething anger, she aimed to achieve a steady, reasonable tone. 'Must I really outline the obvious—or is it a case of a shocking incident ceasing to become shocking when it becomes a familiar activity?'

'Shocking incident? Last night, d'you mean . . .?' His hoot of derisive laughter was confirmation, if she had needed it, that any attempt to impose moral judgment upon such a man would be as punitive as trying to slap a bridle on a creature of the wilds.

'Come now, Kate,' he jeered, with mockery curling his lips, 'you'll be telling me next that your aunt wasn't joking when she bracketed you with Victorian maidens who wore bonnets with ribbons tied beneath the chin, who linked chastity with modesty and tried to cultivate an illusion that, like cherubs, no body existed from the neck downwards!'

Resentful of being made to feel a figure of fun, she countered stiffly, 'Obviously you've strayed well out of your accustomed territory. Here in Shetland, chastity has not yet become outmoded.'

Oblivious to her urge to smack his taunting face, he continued to aggravate. 'But you cut free from social taboos and religious intolerance and chose instead to live in the more modern, free-thinking atmosphere that's made university halls of residence notorious. Was it there that you learnt the art of seduction,' he mused, inching closer, 'how to wear skin-tight denims over slinky hips and shirts two sizes too small that show a tantalising amount of cleavage? You baited the trap with all the traditional titbits of desirability, Kate, which is why I find it hard to understand your adverse reaction, your implication that I'd misread your signals. In my book, any desirable female willing to venture unchaperoned into a tribe of lusty males must be up for grabs!'

Goaded beyond the bounds of discretion, she snapped, 'How was I to know that your favourite choice of reading is *The Jungle Book*!' Fighting a weakness that swamped her when his hovering lips teased a short breath nearer, she croaked, 'One of the theories I learnt while working as secretary to a professor of psychology is that behaviour is determined not so much by an individual's own personality as by the standards and expectations of the society in which he has lived. Beasts are more to be pitied than condemned,' she charged bitterly, 'for beasts can't reason, they're entirely motivated by impulses and urges to seek pleasure in sensual, unrestrained and totally uncivilised activities!'

When his head snapped back she felt pierced by eyes glinting hard amber resentment of the insult. Instinctively she shrank from his aggressive attitude, casting the same look of appeal as a cornered, timid animal offering its throat to an adversary. For a second Leon seemed certain to decide upon the death stroke, but then his ferocious look faded and with it his threat of retaliation.

'Until I met you, Kate, I thought I knew what little a man needs to know about women,' he admitted softly, 'but you're such a confusing mixture of childish innocent and seductive sinner that I never know quite where I am with you—which is why, for a little while longer, I've decided to give you the benefit of the doubt. Meanwhile, don't push your luck too far,' he glinted dangerously. 'Forget your impossible theories about equality of the sexes and dwell instead upon their differences. Millions of years ago Nature cast man in the tough, dominant mould of a hunter born to provide. Then she designed woman as his mate, making her soft, shapely, and appealing so as to ensure that the human race would survive. Nature's command must be obeyed, Kate,' he murmured, leaning to stroke a featherlight kiss across downcast lids. 'Your basic instincts haven't changed—*nor have mine*!'

When his lips swooped to plunder she willed her tremulous mouth to freeze, her traitorous body to resist passionate caresses it had been taught to crave. Impassive as a statue she lay in his arms, green eyes seething with resentment behind a barrier of lowered lashes, her Viking pride outraged at the thought of being considered gullible enough to be duped by a line so well used the words had dripped from his lips like molten honey.

With only one of his arguments she had no dispute. He *was* a hunter, one whose pride had been piqued, whose curiosity had been aroused by the only prey that had managed to elude his net. If stage one of his plan had worked he would not have hesitated to send her packing; if she had succumbed to stage two he would have waved her goodbye at the airport, delegating her to the ranks of the numerous other unfortunates who had been beguiled, bewildered and finally bowled over by his virile, audacious seduction. But because she had resisted, had defeated him at every turn, his conceit would not be satisfied until victory had been won.

When he raised his head and slid his arm from around her shoulders she remained still, expecting a spate of condemnation, but he surprised her with the sighed acceptance,

'You're right, Kate, it's neither the time nor the place. To achieve an act of perfection the stage must be properly set, with a musical prelude to set the mood, comfortable surroundings, dim lighting to create an atmosphere of intimacy and a locked door to act as a barrier against an intrusive world. We never seem to manage more than a quick grope in a dark corner, you and I,' his grin widened at the sight of her scandalised expression. 'My fault entirely, I admit. Take a memo, Miss Dunross,' he teased, totally unrepentant. 'From Casson to Casson—chicks hatch quicker inside a feathered love nest!'

Wishing that Nature had indeed provided her with a pecking beak and scratching talons, Catriona turned her head aside as he drove on, too angry to look at, much less speak to the hard-core chauvinist who seemed to regard her eventual submission as a foregone conclusion.

They arrived at the cottage just in time to see her aunt waving goodbye to the occupants of an ancient Morris being driven by a neighbouring farmer. Catriona noticed immediately that the wrinkled face beneath her Sunday-best bonnet was looking unusually grim and that instead of smiling a welcome her aunt's mouth pursed tightly as she waited for them to join her outside the cottage door. Alert to all the signs and signals, she knew that trouble was brewing when in place of a greeting her aunt nodded downwards, indicating an iron scraper at the edge of the doorstep, then snapped tersely to Leon,

'Clean your boots before you set foot inside!'

To Catriona's amazement he meekly obeyed before following them into the small living-room with curtainless windows and furniture still pulled away from the walls.

'This is a fine state to leave a body in!' she waved an encompassing hand, then spun round to accuse Leon. 'You said you'd be away for only half a day, promised you'd both be back in time for dinner!'

'I'm sorry, Miss Dunross.' Although he had been given leave to address her as Aunt Hanna, even Leon seemed wary of taking liberties when the old lady seemed in such an obviously aggravated mood. 'You must have gone to a lot of trouble yesterday preparing a meal, but owing to bad weather our flight was delayed, so we had to spend the night on the rig.'

'I know you did!' Beneath a black alpaca dress her frail figure seemed to bristle; the knuckles of her hands protruding white through paper-thin skin as she tightened her grip on an ivory-backed prayer-book. 'Also, once gossip has had a chance to circulate, so will half the residents of Shetland! You realise, young man,' her eyes levelled angry accusation, 'that, fiancé or not, you have put my niece's good reputation in doubt?'

'Aunt Hanna!' Catriona protested, appalled. 'That's a ridiculous statement to make!'

'Ridiculous, is it?' Furiously she rounded upon her. 'In that case, it's not me you should be trying to convince but those charitable souls who were circulating the news among the kirk's congregation this morning! I'm casting no doubt upon your morals, child,' momentarily her expression softened, 'nor on yours either, Leon.' Her show of simple trust sent a tide of colour running under his tan. 'You are a true gentleman, I knew the moment you set foot inside my house that Catriona would be safe anywhere with you. Nevertheless,' she continued briskly, 'the word is being spread—its source supposedly some person who was present in the radio room when your message was received at base—that the pair of you have spent the night together! In a community such as ours, the merest whiff of scandal spells death to a girl's chances of marriage. What I want to know,' she swung round to direct her challenge towards Leon, 'is whether you intend taking the only course likely to stop tongues wagging.'

Catriona wanted to shrivel with embarrassment as she waited to see Leon's lips curl upward, to hear him respond with words of mocking ridicule. But a gasp became lodged in her throat when the solemnity of his expression deepened and he responded to her aunt's question with grave courtesy.

'As you so obviously consider me responsible for ruining Kate's reputation, and as I would be deeply upset at the thought of losing either your respect or your friendship, Miss Dunross, I give you my word that I shall willingly follow any course of action you'd care to indicate in order to right what you so obviously consider a grave wrong. What is it that you wish me to do?'

'Announce the date of your wedding, and make it as soon as possible!'

Catriona froze, stunned by words ringing triumphant as a peal of bells. She tried hard to swallow, but her throat was so dry that when she eventually managed to force a protest the only sound that resulted was an incredulous croak, a croak that turned into a choke when after a startled pause she heard his slowly dragged out reply.

'So be it, Miss Dunross. I've already given you my promise, and although my faults are many I take pride in the fact that I've never gone back on my word.'

During the following hour Catriona carried out her tasks in a dazed trance, mechanically laying the table for lunch, listening to sounds of hilarity issuing from the kitchen where her aunt was happily following instructions being given by the stand-back, take-charge guy with a hint of Texas drawl on how to prepare his favourite salad, while he demonstrated the art of making a brand of omelette fit, she heard him assure her giggling aunt, for King Oil and his merry oilmen.

As she sliced and buttered a bannock baked the previous evening—because her aunt insisted that only necessary chores should be undertaken on the Sabbath—she tried to unravel her tangled thoughts, to pinpoint the motive behind Leon's promise which, surprisingly, she did not doubt he was prepared to carry out. Although an undeniable bond of rapport had been forged between himself and her aunt she could not bring herself to believe that his affection for an old lady who had possibly begun to represent the mother he had never known, could be the reason that had prompted him to put his jealously-guarded bachelordom in jeopardy. Again, the notion that he could possibly be concerned about her own reputation being ruined in the eyes of a censorious, sternly moralistic community was dismissed the moment it

was born. Such a situation was more likely to enter-
tain his sense of the ridiculous rather than prick his
rusty, run-down conscience! No, more than likely,
she finally decided with a frown, the insufferably
cocksure, been-everywhere, done-everything Texan
had become bored with his placid existence and
decided to employ her aunt and herself as a form of
amusing diversion.

Having concluded that his intentions were strictly
dishonourable, Catriona found it hard to join in the
conversation that developed into a game of verbal
ping-pong between Leon and her aunt immediately
they all sat down at the table.

'Where did you learn to cook like this, my boy?
Such a delicious omelette!'

'Oh, in ranch cookhouses, and platform galleys,
but mostly over campfires set as far apart as Texas,
Mexico, Alaska and the Arabian Gulf,' he told her
in a lazy drawl.

'What a shame, I thought I detected a woman's
guidance behind your expertise.' Aunt Hanna
sounded slightly disappointed. 'I began teaching
Catriona to cook when she was a mere child, and
now I'd defy anyone in Shetland to better her soused
herrings or cream crowdies,' she boasted, obviously
anxious that he should be made fully aware of his
future good fortune.

'I'll look forward to sampling some of Kate's
cooking.' Catriona kept her gaze concentrated upon
her plate, but knew from his deep-throated chuckle
that he had noted her slow rise of colour. 'You must
invite me to supper soon, darling,' he teased in a
much more gentle manner than she had come to

expect of him. 'I enjoy trying the local delicacies in whichever country I happen to be working.'

She struggled to overcome her confusion, conscious of her aunt's puzzled stare, and felt almost grateful towards Leon when he made a deliberate bid for her aunt's attention.

'I've tried kangaroo soup in Australia; sautéed lizard in South America; bear steaks in China——'

'Leon, stop,' Aunt Hanna pleaded, covering up her ears, 'before you ruin my appetite! I'd imagined that your culinary inclinations would run along the lines of barbecued buffalo steaks.'

'No, ma'am,' smiling broadly, he shook his head, 'there's still more beef eaten in Texas than any other state, but the huge herds of buffalo that once roamed the West are a long time gone and the few that survive are protected by law.'

'But do cowboys still make camp under the open sky, with just a blanket, a rifle, a coffee pot and a handful of hard biscuits?' she asked eagerly. 'And do they still ride the range and have heifer roasted whole on a spit for dinner at sundown, as they did in a film I once saw in a picture house in Lerwick many years ago?'

He grinned widely, seemingly highly amused. 'That film must have been about the rough-and-ready frontier days, Aunt Hanna. Today, cowboys are more likely to be found riding herd in a car than on horseback. But I dare say there might still be a few of the old frontier customs such as hog-calling contests, square dances and cowboy-singing jamborees still to be found. Tell you what . . .'

Catriona's hackles rose when he bent his fiery head

closer to her enthralled aunt as if to impart a confidence of extra special significance.

'. . . how would it be if, once Kate and I are married, I take you both on a visit to Texas? I'd sure enjoy escorting you personally to a rodeo.'

Catriona jumped to her feet, unable to bear another second of his deliberately cruel bolstering of an old lady's excited expectations.

'Don't be tempted to expose your romantic notions to the cold chill of reality, Aunt Hanna,' she rebuked coldly, 'otherwise you'll risk the disappointment of discovering that your cowboy hero of long ago is one of a diminished species and that the legendary home of stetson-wearing cattle barons, round-ups, and flapjacks "rustled up" over open fires has been superseded by rows of ugly oil derricks pumping fluid gold out of stretches of barren wasteland!'

Suddenly, for some indefinable reason totally unconnected with the quiver disturbing her aunt's downcast mouth, or the hard, warning glitter in amber eyes, she knew she was going to cry. Hurriedly she kicked aside her chair and rushed out of the cottage in search of fresh, clean air.

A vigorous gust of wind knocked her breathless the moment she unlatched the kitchen door—just a summer breeze compared to the gale force winter blows that swept the exposed islands treeless—yet powerful enough to rock her on her heels, forcing her to brace before continuing her headlong rush across the small cobbled courtyard harbouring a row of ramshackle outhouses once used as stables and cattle byres but which had been left empty and neglected for many years.

Tears began pouring down her cheeks when, after gaining the sanctuary of a place filled with happy childhood memories, she sagged against a wall and closed her eyes, trying to blot out the present by recalling hours spent tending horses and cattle, crushing oil cake, mashing boiled 'neeps', carrying pails of water and humping bales of straw, watching fascinated while her aunt, seated upon a small, three-legged stool and with her head planted firmly against the flanks of a grateful milch cow, extracted a stream of rich creamy milk that had filled up a pail with amazing speed.

For the first time ever she felt a yearning for the return of days of uncomplicated living when each morning she had been able to look forward to a placid undemanding routine devoid of fears and doubts, sudden shocks, and the sort of emotional upheaval that sent her spirits one minute soaring and the next zooming to zero, a happy state of euphoria that had been abruptly dispelled by the advent into her life of Leon Casson! What was he up to? she wondered, biting a fretful bottom lip. He had blackmailed her into agreeing to a bogus engagement, had forced her to submit to the indignity of being used as a decoy fiancé because he had become weary of being made the target of gossip, tired of having his love life analysed, and subjected to constant speculation. But what on earth had possessed him to allow the deception to go beyond the point of no return? Why had he agreed to settle a definite date for a bogus wedding, even going so far as to cruelly buoy up the hopes of her unsuspecting aunt with an invitation to America which he knew could never be implemented.

'. . . *once Kate and I are married!*'

Feeling pain so intense it forced from her lips a gasped sob, she sagged down in a stricken, bewildered heap upon a mattress of discarded straw.

She wept until her reservoir of misery had run dry, then rolled over on her back to lie staring up at the raftered ceiling, her eyelids red and swollen, her mouth a trembling, punished victim of woe.

'I read once in the Bible that they who sow in tears shall reap in joy!'

When Lèon's shadow fell across her face she remained very still, resentful of his intrusion into a mood of resigned yet peaceful despair. Conscious of his demanding stare, she responded woodenly,

'From that monument of English prose one can always pick out a text here and there and make it serve our purpose. At this moment, I can think of one particular quotation that reads like a personal warning: "Be sober, be vigilant; because your adversary the devil, as a roaring lion, walketh about, seeking whom he may devour".'

The straw rustled as he eased his fluid limbs down beside her. Tension tightened her nerves as she waited expectantly for him to exercise his satanic prerogative of always insisting upon having the last word.

But the low, sober tone of his voice, the fact that he attempted no physical assault upon prey so wounded, so obviously at his mercy, took her by surprise, made her feel that an abyss had yawned at her feet, leaving her teetering on a rim of uncertainty.

'Do you really consider me to be such a son of a bitch that I'd find pleasure in baiting a very lovable old lady?'

Catriona ought to have found it easy to respond with a prompt affirmative, but for some unaccountable reason she merely twisted her head round and stared at the rangy, unsmiling Texan who deserved every scornful insult she ached to fling his way yet whose unguarded look of dejection had reminded her for one split second of the barefooted, freckle-faced urchin to whom Geoff had once likened him.

'If so, you've got me all wrong, Kate,' he continued plucking at her heartstrings. 'Just lately I've been coming around to Geoff's way of thinking, have begun wondering whether the chains of married bondage weigh less heavy than those of single loneliness. In any case, I've decided to give matrimony a try. I promised your aunt that I'd marry you, Kate—she's now making arrangements for the minister to call so that we can decide upon a mutually convenient date for the wedding to take place.'

CHAPTER TEN

'I'm so looking forward to tonight's jamboree, Catriona,' Sandra confided happily. 'The whole base is humming with excitement. We all love it when the American contingent arrange one of their special Country and Western dances, but the fact that we have all been invited to celebrate your engagement to Leon is a bonus that's escalated anticipation to fever pitch. Have you decided yet what you'll be wearing?' she prattled on, too wrapped up in envisaging her own party outfit to notice Catriona biting nervously into her bottom lip, or to see a look in her eyes akin to despair.

'I have a dress that might be appropriate.' Her struggle to eliminate all trace of bitterness from her tone resulted in a flat, even monotone far removed from the joyful response expected of a newly engaged girl delighted by the prospect of standing at the side of her fiancé accepting happy congratulations. 'A red and white gingham discarded years ago when it became unfashionable, that I've smartened up with a few yards of broderie anglaise so as to project the image of shy, wholesome womanhood reputedly favoured by Texas cowboys.'

Sandra stopped sorting through a pile of invoices to cast a glance of amusement towards Catriona's regal head crowned by a flaxen coronet, bent closely over a typewriter.

'I can't quite picture you wearing a poke bonnet and controlling a team of horses from the seat of a covered wagon,' she grinned, 'but Leon fits exactly my image of a gun-totin', hard-riding, early frontiersman who viewed uncharted territory as a challenge, who fought hard and lived dangerously because he was one of a unique breed of men who liked nothing better than to be given an opportunity to prove themselves capable of taming the untameable.'

Heaving an exasperated sigh, Catriona abandoned a halfhearted attempt to clear up a backlog of items that had been pushed aside, left to gather dust during the past hectic weeks when they had been delegated relatively unimportant.

'I suspect you read too many trashy Westerns,' she reproved the unabashed teenager. 'I refuse to sit here another minute listening to such drivel. In fact, I think I'll call it a day.' She glanced down at her watch, then rose to her feet with a look of decision. 'Since I've worked hours of overtime recently, I don't consider anyone is likely to object to my taking a little time off. If Leon should question my absence,' she told Sandra, who looked on astonished when she began shrugging on her coat, 'tell him that I decided to leave for home an hour early.'

Defiance continued smouldering while she was being driven in a company car towards her aunt's cottage, staring out of the window at clouds banking dark and heavy as her mood, a dull grey blanket of depression lowering over a smooth sheet of sea that looked ominously calm in spite of a coppery tinge on the far horizon and an occasional low grumbling of

thunder. But it was her own inner storm of temper
that was holding her attention, the impotent frustration of being made to feel used, of having had every
vehement objection overruled by a man who had
decided on an arrogant whim to *'give matrimony a
try'*.

But this time he had stretched her patience too
far. An impulse prompted by the shock of discovering, upon her arrival at work that morning, that in
spite of her stated refusal to take him seriously he
had deliberately spread news of his matrimonial intentions around the entire workforce and had even
arranged for a celebration to take place that same
evening, had developed during the day into a definite course of action. The deception she had initially
regarded as harmless was getting out of hand, so
much so that she was now left with no alternative
but to tell her aunt the truth.

It was barely four o'clock when the car drew up
outside of the cottage, yet already it was dark enough
to justify the lamp casting a welcoming glow through
small square windowpanes. When quietly Catriona
opened the door and stepped into the living-room
she saw her aunt sitting in a chair pulled close up to
a table so that light from an oil lamp was falling
directly upon what appeared to be a pile of white
gauze heaped upon her lap. When her aunt's head
remained bowed, she spoke gently to break her
absorption.

'Aunt Hanna, I thought we'd agreed that you
were to give up any close work that might damage
your eyesight?'

Immediately her aunt became aware of her presence her guilty start dislodged the material on her lap so that a ray of light glistened upon a steel crocheting needle positioned between gnarled fingers.

'What on earth are you doing?' Catriona darted forward, concerned by the obvious weakness of eyes peering in her direction.

'Ah, well,' her aunt sank back into her chair with a resigned sigh, 'now that I've been caught out I might as well admit that for many months past I've been working on your wedding dress.'

'My wedding dress? But until yesterday the subject of my marriage had never arisen!'

'Nevertheless,' the old lady smiled, 'it was inevitable that one day you *would* marry, and as time is getting short, and work of this nature can't be accomplished in weeks, nor even months, I decided that it was time to begin putting my house in order.'

'I don't understand.' Thoroughly bewildered, Catriona dropped to her knees at the side of her aunt's chair and ran wondering fingers over gossamer-light wool, pale as milk, exquisitely fashioned into a dress as light and ethereal as a floating cloud.

'Well, what do you think of it, child?' her aunt prompted eagerly. 'You'll need to wear a plain white petticoat beneath, of course, otherwise it wouldn't be decent, but I think it's turned out quite nicely, don't you?'

'Quite nicely!' Faintly, Catriona echoed the understatement, momentarily lost for words. 'It's *adorable, exquisite,* simply out of this world,' she choked, 'yet I dread to think of the strain such a task must have inflicted upon your eyes!' She swallowed hard to disperse a lump in her throat, then continued more sternly, 'Also, I'm puzzled by your remark about putting your house in order.'

With a smile sweeter than any Catriona had ever previously seen, her aunt reached out to cup her distressed face between calloused palms and reprimanded gently,

'Kate, my dear, you must try to accept the fact that my future is limited—at any rate, on this earth. Whenever the subject has arisen you've insisted upon pushing it aside, which is perhaps understandable, for the thought of dying is often more uncomfortable to the young than to the old. But don't misconstrue my wish to discuss the matter freely and openly as an implication that death is imminent—it's merely inevitable. I've reached the age when the prospect of completing life is no longer frightening, which is why I'm trying to ensure that all is in order, that when you walk down the aisle towards your bridegroom everyone present will envy him his hauntingly lovely bride.' She lifted a hand to dash a tear from her cheek then returned to her usual brisk manner. 'And now, as you've obviously returned home early in order to give yourself plenty of time to prepare for the evening's festivities we'd better dally no longer. I'm so looking forward to the party,' she heaved an ecstatic sigh. 'It's many, many years since I last attended a celebration!'

Alone in her bedroom a couple of hours later, Catriona stared into her mirror, feeling trapped and bemused as her wide eyed reflection. Despising herself for her cowardice, for her weak disinclination to wipe the stars from her aunt's eyes, to force her brave soul to endure yet another bitter disappointment, she appealed to her accusing image.

'I hadn't the heart to spoil her evening. But I'll tell her the truth tomorrow,' she promised herself. 'After all, keeping my own counsel for a few hours longer can make very little difference.'

Though her reflected expression remained accusing she continued staring into the mirror at the figure dressed in a sweetly simple fashion that made her appear incapable of deception, given a flushed, appealing, country-girl look by a dress of red and white checked gingham with a sweetheart neckline cut just low enough to reveal a discreet amount of cleavage; a tightly nipped-in waist, and a widely flaring skirt with a glimpse of lace-trimmed petticoat peeping beneath the hem.

Stifling a sob, she closed her eyes, trying to shut out thoughts of what it might be like to be married to the man whom Sandra had likened to a romantic folk hero, one of the self-reliant, drinking, fighting, argumentative, reckless pioneers who had opened up the West, swilling beer and Bourbon and bedding every fanciable girl they met along the way. How was it possible, she wondered, for a country's habits and customs to change yet for its menfolk to remain basically the same? Pioneers were an extinct species; cowboys had been enticed from ranches by lucrative oilfields, yet Leon Casson was still lassoing and breaking in steers, getting his kicks from branding his mark upon the pick of the herd!

'Catriona!' Her aunt's voice hailing her from below jerked her back to painful reality. 'Leon has arrived, are you ready, my dear?'

Casting a last look at her demure reflection,

Catriona swung away from the mirror, regretting the impulse that had led her to leave her hair unplaited, brushed to the sheen of a shimmering veil, then swept apart at the nape of her neck to be gathered and held by two bright red ribbons. Snatching up a small white purse, she hurried out of the room, then jolted to a standstill halfway down the stairs when she saw Leon watching her descent as he waited in the hall-way.

She blushed, suddenly overwhelmed by shyness, then forced her reluctant feet to progress slowly towards the man whose intent amber eyes were tracing a low, possessive course along every curve of her body, resenting the leap of senses startled out of control by the sight of whip-lean limbs clad in traditional Western outfit of slim-cut Levis, a black pearl-buttoned shirt with collar falling away over a colourful neckerchief, handstitched leather boots and, what appealed to her shattered confidence, the last aggressive straw, a wide-brimmed Stetson tipped to the back of his arrogant head.

'Well,' he drawled slowly, 'I'm glad to see that you've entered into the spirit of things, Kate! You look great, all set for a night of belt 'n buckle polishin' music.'

Her blush deepened as, keeping her eyes fixed upon his silver belt buckle, she jerked defensively, 'Please don't flatter yourself that I've dressed up for your benefit—this "Come Dancing" outfit,' she cast a disparaging glance at her gingham skirt, 'was Aunt Hanna's idea and when Sandra confirmed that such do's are usually thronged with boutique cowboys escorting crinolined Annie Oakleys I saw no reason why my aunt shouldn't be given an opportunity to live out her fantasy. You see, she clings to the naïve assumption that modern-day Texans are true counterparts of those protective, female-cosseting heroes she once saw portrayed on the silver screen—quick-shooting Sir Galahads who would duel to the death to protect their womenfolk's virtue.'

During the bitter silence that fell like a barrier between them she dared not look up, but kept her eyes fixed in the region of his flat midriff watching stomach muscles knot beneath a shirt stretched smooth as pelt as he drew in a sharp, enraged breath. A clock ticking slowly and inevitably as blood that seemed squeezed in drops from her constricted heart was the only sound disturbing the silence that was suddenly shattered by a harshly grated question.

'And how do *you* feel about Texans, Kate? Obviously you're not in sympathy with your aunt's opinion?'

'My aunt has not been herded, lassoed and hogtied as I have,' she tilted scornfully, glancing upwards to where a pulse of strong emotion was hammering against his jutting jaw.

'Damned ornery critters just ask to be handled rough!' he snapped, just a split second before his vicious grip descended upon her shoulders. 'You're a maverick, Kate, forever kicking against capture, but there's one other thing you ought to know about Texans—once he's slipped a rope around the neck of a critter, nothing in creation will make him let go!'

Viciously, she was jerked against his chest, then, searing as a branding iron, his mouth descended upon hers, melting words of resentment from her lips, forcing her head backward until it was steadied against his arm while he plunged deeper and deeper until she felt the imprint of his punishing mouth had been branded upon her heart.

When he lifted his head she was too shocked to speak, her senses numbed—as flesh appears numb upon first contact with flame, before the inevitable onset of throbbing, unbearable pain.

'I want you to wear this tonight.' She was incapable of resistance when he loosened his grip to jerk her hand upwards to slide a cold, hard band around her finger. For a second she gazed dully at the unfamiliar object, then when realisation dawned she lifted her head to communicate contemptuous dislike with eyes that were glistening, dark, depthless green as the emerald ring lying heavy as a fetter upon her finger.

'There you both are!' Aunt Hanna appeared clutching a soft Shetland shawl around her best alpaca dress. 'I'm ready when you are. And by the way, Leon, I hope you've remembered your promise to arrange transport home for me? Much as I'm looking forward to this party, I know I shall be ready to leave after an hour—two at the very most.'

'There's a driver on stand-by duty,' he assured her, courteously offering her his arm, 'he'll be ready and waiting to drive you back home immediately you say the word.'

Employing the ruse of insisting that her aunt would be much more comfortable travelling in the front passenger seat, Catriona managed to avoid close proximity with the man whose trampling over her emotions she deeply resented, who threw her into such confusion that even while she sat behind him nursing her hatred, every off-guard moment found her eyes straying towards his wood-chipped profile, watching the way his lips curled up at the edges whenever he was amused, tracing his dark underscore of eyebrows and thick tangled lashes, straining her ears to catch the affectionate cadences of his voice when he spoke to her aunt—feeling aghast when she recognised a strange, spearing emotion as envy!

When she walked by his side into the spacious building with an interior that had been transformed overnight to resemble a barn made to look cosy with occasional bales of hay stacked into corners; trestle tables covered with bright chequered cloths and an array of food sufficient to feed an army of hungry oilmen; coloured lights festooned around walls lined with benches packed with smiling guests, no one was allowed to guess that her dignified, rather cool exterior was hiding a pounding, racing, panic-stricken stampede of nerves.

As if taking their cue from the cheers that had greeted their arrival, a band of check-shirted musicians launched into a steady, guitar-twanging, foot-tapping rhythm that drew a stream of dancers on to the chalk-strewn floor—a cross-section of workers ranging from middle-class accountants to humble labourers who had all indulged in a favourite fantasy by turning out in designer jeans, lizard-hide boots, decorative belts and wide-brimmed hats lined with leather sweat-band, each partnering pretty girls wearing short, crinolined dresses.

'Well, what are you waiting for?' Aunt Hanna urged brightly. 'Don't bother about me, go right ahead and join in the dancing.'

Immediately, Catriona recoiled a step backwards. 'I couldn't, I wouldn't know how to begin!'

Swift as a snakebite, Leon's fingers clasped her wrist and with a smile that challenged her to physically resist in front of their interested audience, he insisted smoothly,

'Then now is as good a time as any to learn!'

Given no chance to protest, she was swept into the circle of dancers, twirled around until her back was positioned directly in front of Leon's chest, then with his right hand decorously clasping hers from across her shoulder he began initiating her into the nimble, high-prancing steps of a square dance.

For the first few minutes she was tense with nervousness, very conscious of his muscled chest pressing like a buffer against her shoulderblades, of his hands sliding downwards to span her waist without apparent effort, of his breath brushing past her flushed cheek, cool as mint, yet intimate as a caress. But as gradually she began mastering the intricacies of the dance shyness was replaced by a surge of enjoyment that enabled her to spin and twirl and curtsey and prance while barely conscious of her grinning partner or the many pairs of eyes closely following her progress.

Leon's grin quickly faded, however, when as soon as the dance had finished and another was due to begin she was besieged by a horde of fun-loving oilmen determined to claim the privilege of dancing with their boss's future bride. Looking flushed and bewildered, she stood within a circle of would-be partners, watching Leon being elbowed aside, almost deafened by the clamour of urgent invitations.

'Clear off, all of you!' When a decisive voice thundered over the heads of her persistent admirers its familiar tone sent her head jerking round. Pleasure and happiness transformed her expression as she extended welcoming hands towards the man cutting a swathing advance through the crowd.

'Geoff!' she greeted him with shining eyes. 'What are you doing here, why aren't you out on the rig?'

'I'm due a spell off duty,' he grinned. 'Flew in half an hour ago and came straight here to join in the celebration and to offer my very best wishes for your future happiness, my dear.'

As the smile died upon her lips at this reminder of trouble to come, Leon appeared at Geoff's side his frown graduating into a full-blown glower that ought to have served as a warning to Geoff to tread carefully.

'Thanks for the good wishes,' he acknowledged curtly, 'but now that you've said your piece you can cut off home and see your family.'

'Not likely,' Geoff refused, quite unabashed. 'In common with the rest of the guys present, I intend taking full advantage of the only opportunity we've had to snatch a pretty girl from under your nose. You can keep her to yourself once you're married,' he grinned, 'but tonight she belongs to all of us!'

When for dance after dance Catriona was claimed by a different partner it soon became obvious that the boisterous oilmen had hatched a mischievous conspiracy to keep herself and Leon apart. Even her aunt noticed and remarked upon it when, just as she was preparing to leave, she signalled a summons across the dance floor.

'I'm going home now, child. No need to ask if you're enjoying yourself,' she swept a look over Catriona's exhilarated face, 'the fact is self-evident. I suspect, however, that Leon is furious and I can't say that I blame him. In my young days,' she sniffed, 'it simply wasn't done for an engaged girl to be seen dancing all night with any man other than her fiancé!'

'Goodnight, Aunt Hanna.' Too relieved to be rid of Leon's company to pretend any show of penitence, she smiled as she stooped to kiss her aunt's cheek. 'Go right upstairs to bed, don't you dare wait up for me, I feel like dancing until dawn.'

'There's a saying: "The morning is wiser than the evening",' her aunt responded tartly. 'Let's hope that when a new day dawns you'll not be called upon to acknowledge that a dram of discretion is worth a pound of wisdom!'

Champagne corks were popping all around when Leon finally managed to run her to ground. Dismissing her companion with a frosty look, he grabbed her wrist and simmered dangerously,

'Geoff is about to propose a toast. As you appear to have forgotten, I thought I'd better remind you that we're engaged to be married—and supposedly in love.'

Catriona shivered, her elated spirits zooming. 'I hadn't forgotten. However, now that Aunt Hanna has had her little bit of fun, there's something I must tell you. I've decided——'

'Yes, carry on, what have you decided?' he

prompted when she faltered, stunned by the realisation that it was not going to be as easy as she had anticipated to confess to the arrogant oil boss that even before the party had commenced she had decided to call his bluff, to make him appear to have been jilted in the eyes of employees and friends. The enormity of her crime was reflected in her wide-eyed look of panic when she begged.

'Is there somewhere where we can talk in private, I must . . .'

But her last words were drowned by a roll of drums that sounded in her ears like a prelude to the guillotine, a fate that loomed larger when Geoff's commanding voice boomed a laughing command through a microphone.

'Friends, this is the moment we've all been waiting for, the official declaration that the wiliest bachelor in camp has finally relinquished his jealously guarded freedom! Raise your glasses and join me in a toast to the newly-engaged couple—Catriona and Leon. I wish them not just a good marriage, but a delightful, friendly loving relationship!'

For the following hour she was leashed to Leon's side with a grip that refused to be prised from her waist even though the teasing conspiracy to keep them apart had ceased with the official announcement of his right of possession. She endured the nightmare of pretence, the jokes and hearty congratulations with a smile pinned to her lips and an air of reticence which, because there are few visible signs of clammy palms and hammering heartbeats, was put down to shy confusion.

Leon, his good humour completely restored,

seemed to have forgotten her urgent request to talk privately, for once they had completed a tour of the room and shaken hands with everyone present, he began guiding her in the direction of the buffet.

'You must be hungry.' Her pulses reacted with a leap to his look of concern.

'I couldn't eat a thing,' she refused hastily. 'Please, Leon, can we go somewhere and talk now?'

'Not until you've sampled some traditional American food,' he refused gravely. 'The wives of men stationed on the base have gone to a great deal of trouble preparing a buffet dinner at very short notice, you can't leave without showing your appreciation. We Westerners are a blunt, uncomplicated crowd who have little use for frills either in food or behaviour, we prefer substance to style and like nothing better than "pot luck" with unexpected guests, which is probably why the buffet dinner has become a symbol of our code, which is,' he bent to whisper closely into her ear, 'that every man should take as much as he wants, as often as he wants—and that a woman should always hold plenty in reserve!'

Scarlet-cheeked, she accompanied him in silence towards tables laden with hams, chicken, pork, pies, salads and fritters, cookies, jellies, jams and chocolate cake, and accepted without further demur the piled-up plate of food he insisted on providing, though she knew that even the tiniest morsel would lodge in her constricted throat. As she watched him tucking into a plateful of spare ribs she attempted to distract his attention from her own lack of appetite with a feeble jest.

'I know you Texans have earned the reputation of

being hearty eaters, but I'd imagined I was having my leg pulled when someone assured me that cowboys have appetites so immense they tie sides of bacon to their feet and use them like skates to grease the griddle before cooking their breakfast pancakes. Were you brought up to regard a laden table as a symbol of success, a reward for honest work?'

To her surprise she saw a shadow cross his features as he turned aside to dispose of his empty plate.

'When I was a child, food was never plentiful in our household,' he told her bleakly, 'which is probably why I view waste not so much as a crime but a sin. I learnt how to become an expert beggar, how to cultivate an expression of pathos guaranteed to cajole meals from the mothers of school friends, and to reward them with a show of gratitude. As a consequence, I grew up with a burning ambition to succeed,' he grated the admission, 'so that I would never again be called upon to don a mask of humility.'

A mask that's been replaced by an armour of pride, Catriona almost blurted to the man she was about to jilt, the man who reacted with a lion's snarl to even the smallest sting!

'I think we can safely slip away now without the danger of being missed,' Leon suddenly surfaced from his retrospective mood to cast a look of tolerant amusement around the room full of noisy revellers. 'As you're obviously anxious to discuss some problem, I suggest the best place to talk would be my trailer where we'll run no risk of being interrupted.'

She hesitated, torn between a desire to be free of deception and fear of being devoured by anger in the solitude of his den.

'Very well,' she gulped, succumbing to the folly of desperation, 'what I have to say won't take longer than a few minutes.'

She almost changed her mind when, after slipping unobtrusively from the hall, she saw the night sky tinged with the first pale light of dawn but stifled an impulse to run back to the warmth and safety of the crowded room and allowed him to steer her swiftly towards the perimeter of the camp where his isolated trailer was situated. As he fumbled in the dark to fit the key into the lock she drew nervously away, but as if sensing her instinct to run he opened the door, then turned swiftly to grab her elbow and propel her in front of him up the steps of the trailer.

She stumbled across the threshold, then gasped with surprise when, at the click of a switch, light flooded a spacious, luxuriously equipped interior.

'Make yourself comfortable.' He waved her towards a plumply upholstered banquette couch covered with oyster velvet, then dimmed the lights to a soft warm glow before striding across to a drinks cabinet. 'What can I get you to drink?'

'Nothing, thank you,' she jerked, her courage dragging heavily as her feet through thick pile carpet.

'Very well,' he swivelled towards a hi-fi cabinet, 'then how about a little background music? Have you a favourite choice that might be appropriate?'

'Appropriate to what?' She shrank nervously towards the couch.

'It all depends,' he responded smoothly, moving swiftly to join her immediately she sat down, 'whether you wish to employ the power of music to soften rocks or bend a knotted oak, or to use it as an opiate to dull pricks of prudish conscience.'

The touch of his fingers stroking a sensuous caress against the sensitive nape of her neck sent her jerking out of reach until there was a yard of ominous, pulsating space between them. Unbearably agitated by the realisation that she had been foolish to trust herself alone with him, she jumped to her feet and began backing towards the door.

'Come here, Kate,' he commanded softly, patting the empty space beside him.

'Not without a chair and a whip,' she lashed out, terrified. 'I didn't come here to be mauled, I came to tell you that I intend telling Aunt Hanna the truth. Here . . .!' She snatched the ring from her finger and threw it at his feet. 'I won't wear your ring, and I refuse to be used as a sort of . . . of . . . guineapig in your matrimonial experiment!'

He leapt towards her with such swift fluidity she had no time to do more than catch a terrified breath before he pinned her with her back against a wall and held her quivering beneath the force of his physical anger.

'I promised your aunt that we would marry, and I intend keeping that promise,' he menaced tightly. 'Gossiping tongues must be stilled.'

'Did you seriously believe I'd allow myself to be blackmailed into marriage by the threat of further idle speculation?' she scoffed, attempting to wriggle free of his punishing grip. 'Gossip soon dies when it is given nothing to feed upon!'

'In that case,' he responded thickly, jerking her hard against his chest to pin her upturned face with an amber bright gleam of determination, 'we must begin here and now to prepare a banquet! The news that we've spent what's left of the night together should suffice as a tasty starter!'

'You wouldn't be such a beast!' she choked.

Deliberately, cruelly, expertly, he seduced her into silence with kisses that left her in no doubt that so far as he was concerned gossip had not lied when it had likened him to the ruthless, merciless hot-blooded king of the jungle.

Torrid moments later she had been reduced to a clinging, helpless state of abandon, transported in Leon's arms to the steaming heat of a tropical paradise where the air was warm and potent as burgundy, where flowers were drawn out of tight virgin buds to blossom into beautiful maturity, where orchestral waters played unseen behind a sultry screen of privacy guaranteed to tempt timid creatures from their shells to explore the pleasant diversions of connubial bliss.

She was hovering on the brink of surrender, lying totally acquiescent in his arms, when a violent knocking erupted to merge with the frantic thudding of her heartbeats.

'Leon!' She heard Geoff's voice penetrating from behind the closed door. '. . . Are you in there?'

'Go to hell, Geoff!' Succinctly, Leon made plain his resentment of the untimely interruption. 'You've tried that ploy once before, did you really expect it to work as effectively a second time around?'

'Believe me, Leon, this time I'm not kidding!' Geoff sounded desperate. 'You're needed out here— I've just received word that a serious situation has developed out on the rig!'

CHAPTER ELEVEN

Less than half an hour later they were airborne. Looking tight-lipped and exceedingly grim, Leon piloted the helicopter over sea heaving and fretting in the cold light of dawn, flying low to avoid massed banks of cloud stretching without a break towards light glowing like a strip of copper wire across the horizon.

Catriona shivered and snuggled closer into the warmth of borrowed slacks and a thick-knit sweater, feeling numbed not so much by the chilly atmosphere as by the memory of Leon's implacable insistence that she should accompany himself and Geoff out to the rig, treating her as a sort of hostage, she reflected bitterly, because he had been deeply suspicious of Geoff's motives. During the ensuing rush to scramble into warm clothing before racing in his Range Rover towards the heliport there had been time for no more than a staccatoed exchange of words between the two men, from which she had gathered that owing to some mishap two divers appeared to be in danger of losing their lives.

As if conscious of the desolation swamping the tense figure crouched into the seat next to his, Geoff reached out to give her hand a comforting squeeze. They were sitting directly behind Leon who, ever since take-off, had maintained constant radio contact with the men aboard the rig, snapping terse questions and receiving replies that deepened the furrows across his brow, too engrossed and concerned to toss even the briefest of apologies towards Geoff when his suspicions were proved to be unfounded.

'I'm sorry I couldn't persuade Leon to listen to reason, Catriona.' Geoff bent his head closer to avoid having to shout above the noise of the engine. 'He must have realised by now what a fool he was to force you to endure such an uncomfortable and unnecessary journey. I must say that I found his attitude amazing. Never, during the whole of our long and close association, has he proved himself so unamenable to reason.'

'I may be partly to blame,' she shrugged. 'I seem to possess a talent for provoking his anger. Anyway, it doesn't matter now—my discomfort is minor compared with the danger being faced by the divers. Whatever is wrong, do you think we'll be in time to save them?' she queried anxiously.

'If anyone can, Leon will,' he told her, his sombre expression deepening. 'Whichever new technique is employed—and much expertise has been borrowed from astronaut explorers of outer space—he has always insisted upon being the first one to experiment with equipment that has pushed back diving frontiers to an extent that would have been considered unbelievable just a couple of years ago. His argument has always been that he has far less to lose than most—no home, no parents, no wife, not so much as a pet poodle to grieve over his loss—but that argument no longer applies, does it, Catriona?' he urged, sweeping keen eyes over her suddenly stricken face. 'The acquisition of a devoted, loving fiancée has made Leon as vulnerable as the rest of us.'

Tears spurted to her eyes when his words painted a portrait of Leon with a stark, lonely background which had previously remained muted, a canvas daubed heavily with the brush of a feckless woman who had put her own selfish pleasures before the welfare of a child; smudged by the passing of the many light, meaningless affairs which which he had tried, but failed, to fill in yawning gaps of loneliness. As gradually as the veil of cloud making way for golden sunrise awareness dawned, understanding of how a cat that has been continuously kicked will react with a snarl to every approaching footstep, of how a boy starved of love and tenderness could grow up thinking women were cast in the same uncaring, immoral mould as his aunt.

Smothering a small gasp of pain, she turned eyes bright with inner illumination upon Geoff and dispersed his frown by whispering.

'Look after Leon, Geoff—he mustn't be allowed to take unnecessary risks!'

Immediately the outline of the rig appeared on the horizon she was struck by a lack of movement, by the jibs of cranes left bowed as if in prayer, and decks and alleyways that seemed becalmed and bewitched as the ill-fated *Mary Celeste*. The eerie sensation was dispelled when she spotted signs of activity on the helipad where a safety crew was awaiting the landing of the helicopter, but as soon as it touched down and she and Geoff had alighted they were met by an uncanny, brooding silence, contained within an aura of atmospheric tension.

'The platform has been shut down,' he explained briefly, 'and will remain so until the divers have been rescued.'

'This is no time to stand gossiping!' Leon snapped unfairly, jumping down from the cockpit to go striding past. 'Follow me, I've instructed all diving personnel to assemble for a meeting in the control room.'

When they arrived inside the control room Leon took his place behind a paper-strewn desk and glanced keenly around the clutch of grim-faced men hovering with fists clenched deeply inside jacket pockets.

'Now,' he demanded, 'fill me in with every last detail of how the accident happened, why and when.'

Simultaneously, the assembled men swivelled their attention upon one particularly gaunt-looking man as if electing him their spokesman. Squaring his shoulders, he accepted the responsibility.

'The divers were carrying out a routine inspection of the underwater structure yesterday when they came across an anchor cable they suspected might be working loose. The sea was calm at the time, weather conditions ideal, but as a warning had been received that a storm was imminent they were instructed to spend no longer than an hour on the repair. Naturally, as the man in charge, I kept a careful eye on the clock and shortly before the given time I relayed instructions that they were to return to the diving bell. They pleaded to be allowed just ten minutes more, so,' he sighed, running a fretful hand through thinning hair, 'as conditions were still calm and the job was urgent, I gave permission for them to carry on.'

'Stop blaming yourself, Jock,' one of his listeners cut in, 'each one of us would have made the same decision had we been in your shoes. What happened next was totally unexpected, impossible to foresee.' He swung round to assure Leon. 'As Jock has just stated, conditions at the time were what we have come to regard as normal for this area—gusting wind, choppy sea, lots of cloud, but nothing out of the ordinary except perhaps for the band of what we assumed to be clear sky on the far horizon.'

Catriona jerked to attention, reminded of the copper-tinged sky she had noticed on her way home from work the day before, the grumbling of thunder and glass-smooth sea that any islander could have told them were the almost certain harbingers of a freak storm.

'One moment conditions were routine,' Jock continued confirming her theory, 'and the next we seemed to have been hit by a blast of thunderbolts, sheet lightning, and wind that heaved huge waves out of the guts of the sea. Though the storm lasted no longer than ten minutes all hell seemed to have been let loose, and it was during that period that the support vessel shifted so violently that the umbilical cord connecting the ship to the diving bell was severed, leaving the divers trapped on the seabed deprived of vital elements.'

'Is the diving bell's emergency support system working satisfactorily?' Leon questioned swiftly.

'It is,' Jock nodded, 'and has been for almost ten hours now—about half the maximum time.'

'And are you still in contact with the trapped divers?' Leon demanded.

'Thank goodness, yes. So far, their only complaint has been that the standard of food has fallen far below that to which they've become accustomed. But they're still able to breathe normally and an acceptable level of heat is being maintained inside the diving bell.'

Resolutely, Leon rose to his feet. 'Well, men, as pressure can't be guaranteed inside a bell that's leaking, you have obviously concluded that any attempt to winch it to the surface would pose a threat to the divers' safety. The leak can't be a major one, however, otherwise the men would already have begun feeling the onset of hypothermia. But as we're all aware that leaks never improve and invariably worsen, we dare not gamble upon being allowed more than several hours' grace if our rescue operation is to be guaranteed successful.'

He swung his attention upon the man in charge of diving operations, and prompted a kindling of gratitude into his worried eyes by declaring firmly,

'Jock, I'd like you to join me aboard the support vessel. I shall be going down in the rescue bell, and there's no one I'd rather have in charge of the operation.'

'There's just one big drawback to that scheme, Leon,' Catriona heard one man's voice rising above a chorus of dissent, 'we'd have sent a rescue bell down long before now if it were not that the weathermen have firmly vetoed the idea. They insist that, as there are still violent storms in the area, we should await their all-clear before running the risk of complicating the situation further with a second similar accident.'

'That's not a drawback in my book,' Leon dismissed, barely checking his stride towards the door, 'merely a minor aggravation.'

With Geoff's help, Catriona managed to scramble unobserved on to the tender that ferried the group of rock-jawed men across a short stretch of sea to where the support vessel was anchored. Once aboard, she tried to catch up with Leon, but managed no more than a glimpse of his broad shoulders as he strode out of sight down an alleyway.

'Geoff,' she appealed, feeling too hollow inside to attempt to hide tears spurting into her eyes, 'I must speak to Leon before he goes over the side!'

He hesitated, then as if sensing her need to put a lot of things right in a very short time, he slowly conceded,

'I'll take you to him, Catriona, but please don't expect too much, for I doubt whether you'll find him in a receptive mood.'

He began ushering her towards the alleyway down which Leon had disappeared, guiding her past a row of closed doors before drawing to a standstill.

'This is the changing room,' he indicated with a nod, 'wait here a moment until I make sure that he's prepared to spare you a few seconds.'

Alone in the alleyway she braced herself to combat a curt refusal, trying not to dwell upon the fear uppermost in her mind, a fear of losing him that she could not even begin to analyse until she had attempted to make her peace with the man who, because of his conviction that he had the least to lose, had chosen to risk his life carrying out a dangerous mission. Tensely she waited, then darted forward when the door opened and Geoff reappeared.

'Leon's almost ready to leave,' he told her with a pitying look, 'but I've managed to persuade him to speak to you before he goes.'

Conveying her thanks with a look of gratitude, she stepped hurriedly into the room he had just vacated, then pulled up sharp, stunned by the impact of seeing Leon's lean frame looking poured into a black rubber suit, clinging supple as sealskin around long limbs, broad chest, and flat, narrow midriff.

'Well, Catriona, whatever you wish to say please say it quickly,' he ordered brusquely, continuing gathering up various items of equipment.

'I . . .' she began, but had to swallow hard when a lump suddenly lodged in her throat. Sensing his impatience to be gone, knowing that any moment he was liable to brush past and disappear out of her life, possibly for ever, she forced out the admission, 'I just wanted to let you know how much I regret our many past misunderstandings. Perhaps in the future,' she croaked, 'if we each agree to try a little harder, we might manage to achieve a better standard of relationship.'

At least, that would do for a start! whispered a fervent inner voice. *Even man's first progress on the moon was measured in slow, tentative steps!*

When unexpectedly, he strode to close the gap between them, the vibrant animal magnetism projected by the play of muscles beneath a supple black skin snatched all the breath from her body.

'There comes a time in every man's life, Kate,' he

told her unemotionally, 'when he's forced by circumstances to reject the dangerous drug of illusion and to come to terms with reality. Reality, so far as you and I are concerned, is conflict, mistrust, dislike and determined resistance. Reality is the preference you show for Geoff's company, the way your eyes light up in his presence, the fact that whenever I've caught you both unawares you've either been kissing or holding hands. In time I shall probably be able to overcome the reality of being jilted—but if you should decide to cause a rift between Geoff and his loving and very lovable wife, I doubt whether I should ever be able to persuade myself that you deserved to be forgiven!'

Leon had gone, lowered over the side of the vessel inside a small metal bell that sank, heavy as her heartbeats, below the waves. As she stood next to Geoff at the ship's rail, her stricken eyes fastened upon an upsurge of bubbles marking the spot where the diving bell had disappeared, she was swamped by a feeling of desolation almost too great to endure. As usual, they had parted in anger, left floundering in a morass of misunderstanding she had been too astonished to even attempt to deny—if she had been given time to do so.

She shivered, staring at a sea made sluggish by breath-held calm, glowing blood red where it reflected a flame streaked, slowly encroaching stretch of copper sky. She was not conscious of Geoff's close scrutiny, was barely aware of his existence until he heaved a sigh.

'There's much I find puzzling about your love affair, Catriona,' he confessed, sweeping a sympathetic look over a quivering mouth, noting the depth of agony in her green eyes. 'To the majority of people Leon will always remain an enigma, a cussed, intolerant, impossible-to-manipulate guy, but you love him, don't you?'

She jolted round to face him, feeling momentarily shocked, ready to blurt out a denial, but somehow the words would not come, and after a dazed silence during which her tangled emotions became magically unravelled she gasped a shaken acknowledgment that wrung his heart.

'Yes, Geoff, I do love Leon—he'll never know how much!'

When he realised now near she was to tears he flung his arm around her shoulders and urged gruffly,

'Let's go below to the control room where they'll be monitoring the diving bell's progress, there's no sense lingering up here.'

But when he tried to urge her forward she resisted by clutching the rail and peering downward as if desperate to plumb the depths of murky water.

'Geoff, please tell me what's happening down there!'

Sharing her sense of helplessness, her painful feeling of isolation, he tried to ease her anxiety by drawing a brief, simple outline of the divers' predicament.

'The damaged bell is lying on the seabed at a depth of approximately six hundred feet. At such depths it's necessary for divers to change over from breathing air—nitrogen and oxygen—to a mixture of helium and oxygen, because nitrogen under pressure has a narcotic effect and produces a sensation of reckless abandon divers call "rapture of the deep". The use of helium averts this hazard, but unfortunately it has the unpleasant drawback of conducting heat from the body, leaving the divers freezing cold. That's why the umbilical cord is used not only to supply air to the bell but also heat in the form of hot water pumped through pipes, to prevent the divers from becoming hypothermic—in other words, chilling to death.'

He hesitated when he saw her wince, but when her questioning eyes urged him to continue he reluctantly carried on.

'Once the umbilical cord has been severed the divers have to fall back upon the emergency support system inside the bell which is designed to allow a rescue time of twenty-four hours.' When she looked stricken he hastened to console her, 'Don't worry, my dear, Leon will get the divers transferred to the rescue bell in no time at all!'

'Why couldn't you have winched the bell to the surface?' she puzzled. 'That way, the rescue could have been concluded much more quickly.'

'Too risky,' Geoff shook his head. 'When a bell is leaking sudden drastic changes of pressure are apt to occur, which could be fatal. After just an hour spent diving at great depth the gas mixture saturates the divers' blood and body tissues to the point where he needs three days or more in a decompression chamber to bring him back to normal. So you must prepare yourself for a short separation,' he tried to sound jocular, 'for even if Leon should complete the rescue within the next hour, it will be at least three days from now before he's back in circulation.'

A clap of thunder drowned her reply. Startled, their eyes swivelled seaward just in time to see lightning rip a ragged tear across a sky active as a boiling cauldron, streaked with flame, seething with hidden turbulence.

'Quickly, get below!' Almost lifting her from her feet, he hauled her away from the rail when raindrops large as saucers began splaying on to the deck with a force that sounded from below deck like an opening burst of machine-gun fire warning of a full-pitched barrage to come.

'Hell!' The voice of an unseen man exploded just as they reached the threshold of the control room. 'That's all we need. Why couldn't the storm have held off for just another hour longer? Better warn Leon that we're preparing to hoist him back to the surface until the storm has passed over.'

'You'll be lucky!' Catriona just caught the words Geoff breathed under his breath. 'It's my guess that he'll refuse to come up until his mission has been completed.'

Proof that he could read Leon's mind better than anyone else present crackled through a radio receiver seconds after the men had informed Leon of their intention.

'I'll come up when I'm ready!' an almost incomprehensible voice commanded. 'We've reached the sea-bed, but our bell has developed a leaking valve that will have to be repaired before we begin transferring the trapped divers. I'm about to go outside the bell to attempt replacing it with a spare!'

Muttering a violent imprecation, Geoff strode

across the room to shout into the microphone,

'Leon, don't be a fool! There's one helluva storm brewing up here, the Captain's doing his best to hold the ship steady, but there's every chance that your lifeline could also be severed. Come up, man! Far wiser to delay another hour than risk having a second bell adrift on the sea-bed!'

Silence was his only answer. Catriona turned away, digging fingernails deep into her palms as she fought to suppress an hysterical urge to snatch up the microphone and sob a heartbroken message through fathoms of murky water. '*Leon, come up! Please, darling, I love you so . . .!*'

But instead she groped her way to a chair set in a corner at the far end of the control room and curled into a cold, tight ball of fear. For the following hour she was forgotten while, as a tempest raged above deck, while men stood by the winches, chilled and soaked to the skin, while the captain barked demented orders to his crew, while in the control room Geoff and Jock sweated and swore as they monitored Leon's movements, at the same time relaying a continuous flow of encouragement to the trapped divers.

As she waited, she felt cold and weary as if she were accompanying Leon on every step of his dangerously delayed mission to locate and replace a faulty valve in the darkness of freezing, zero-visibility sea with constantly changing currents, conscious all the while that if the support vessel should move his lifeline would snap, depriving him of air and essential heat.

After what seemed an aeon of suspense she heard

Leon's calm, matter-of-fact voice reporting,

'The valve has been repaired and the trapped divers, both in fair conditions, have been transferred to the rescue bell. We're now ready to be winched back to the surface.'

She jumped to her feet, then swayed, aware, as if from a long way away, of the sound of cheering, shouted comments, and tension-ridding laughter, then with a small sigh she slid down to the floor in a relieved faint.

CHAPTER TWELVE

'You'll be getting back to work today, no doubt.'
Aunt Hanna's statement sounded more in the nature
of a command. 'There's nothing more to be done in
here,' she glanced around the small living-room redolent with the smell of fresh paint, gleaming bright
as a new pin with furniture polished to the sort of
sheen only achieved with the aid of plenty of elbow
grease; curtains and covers crisply laundered; rugs
that had been violently attacked with carpet sham-
poo until they had yielded their original pattern of
colours. 'If I didn't know you better, my girl, I'd say
you were using housework as an excuse to delay your
return to the office.'

'Not at all——' Catriona began a protest that was
immediately interrupted.

'Yes, I know you've already explained the circumstances that have kept Leon out of circulation
for a day or two, but surely after a week he must
now be back behind his desk and missing the services
of a secretary?'

Keeping hot cheeks averted from her aunt's scrutiny, Catriona continued polishing the surface of a
table that was already reflecting her features as
clearly as any mirror.

'Perhaps so,' she mumbled, shamed by the knowledge that her aunt's suspicion was not far from the
truth, 'but he knows where I am,' she continued in a

tone with a definite edge, 'so if he wants me, all he needs do is send a message.' She blinked, then had to hastily use her duster to remove all evidence of an escaped tear that was marring the shine on the polished table. Her aunt had not yet been told that during their last encounter Leon had made it plain that he did not want her, nor that his proposal of marriage had been motivated by all the wrong reasons. On several occasions she had been on the verge of explaining, but because the trauma of being closely involved in a mission so dangerous its consequences could easily have been tragic was still fresh in her mind, because the love that had surfaced that day from beneath fathoms of naïveté and wilful blindness was so precious to her—secreted as a pearl inside the shell of an oyster—she had dodged the certainty of an inquisition by allowing her aunt to continue happily putting the finishing touches to her wedding dress, had made no demur when a date had been suggested for the wedding to take place that was less than two weeks away.

'Look here, child,' her aunt sounded as if she were fast losing patience, 'if you are not going into the office, why don't you go *aboot da banks*?—it's a lovely day and the walk will do you good.'

The snatch of ancient dialect brought a glimmer of a smile to Catriona's lips and made the suggestion that she should walk along the edges of the cliffs and down to the beach sound appealing.

'Yes, I think I will,' she decided, her bright head lifting towards sunwarmed windowpanes, 'it's ages since I last went beachcombing on the shore.'

As she was already wearing denims and a cream-coloured jumper with a Fair Isle patterned yolk, she needed only to exchange sandals for a pair of well worn brogues and to sling an anorak over her arm before she was ready. After placing a farewell peck on her aunt's cheek she set off, eager to explore the irregular coastline, the lochs, the hills and dales providing a constant change of scenery that could be fully appreciated only by hiking as far away as possible from the main road.

She had progressed only a couple of hundred yards along an incline leading away from the cottage when her attention was caught by a flashing signal being transmitted by sunshine bouncing off the roof of an approaching car. She stopped to stare towards a bend in the road behind which the car had become hidden, then when it suddenly reappeared speeding swiftly as a silver arrow towards the cottage she took off in panic-stricken flight, hoping to scramble over a nearby ridge before she was spotted by the driver.

But seconds later, the squeal of brakes followed by the sound of a car door slamming told her that the hope had been a vain one. Slowly she turned and waited, quivering with the anxiety of a small, cornered animal who expects to suffer less from the jaws of its trap than from the merciless hands of its trapper.

Purposefully, Leon strode until he was within a couple of feet of where she was standing, then with a gleam she had never before seen in his amber eyes he demanded,

'Why the prolonged absence from the office? Work has piled up to such an extent I've been forced to seek you out. I need help with an important report that must be completed before the end of the week.'

She had wanted so much to see him, to assure herself that he had escaped without injury from his ordeal, nevertheless, the reason that had prompted his appearance goaded her into a snap of temper.

'Robinson Crusoe is the only man I know whose work was all done by Friday!'

To her surprise, he did not bite back with his usual ferocity but responded in the tone of a man determined to remain reasonable, not to be riled.

'Apparently I've been too hard a taskmaster. You're looking pale and your nerves are obviously worn ragged. I'm sorry, Kate,' he astounded her with an apology. 'Your health is more important than any backlog of work, please take as much time off as you feel is necessary to recover from my criminal lack of consideration.' Ignoring her look of surprise, he then took her by the arm and confused her utterly by coaxing, 'As you seem prepared to take a walk, would you mind if I take you up on your offer to share with me the secret pleasures of your island?'

'Less than a minute ago you professed to be snowed under with work,' she reminded him with a show of reluctance that brought a twist of chagrin to his lips.

'And now I've decided to play hookey. I believe in concentrating my mind upon one problem at a time, Kate,' he insisted with a gentleness that scared her more than his usual quick impatience, 'when I'm working I think only about work; when I'm in a mood for play my sole requirement is an agreeable playmate.'

Sensing his determination not to be thwarted, she bowed to the inevitable.

'Very well,' she conceded stiffly, 'what would you like to see first?'

'The wild Shetland ponies I've heard so much about.' Cheerfully, he fell into step beside her. 'I believe they're unique to the islands?'

Immediately, she shied from his close proximity, vitally aware of his rangy, relaxed stride, of limbs supple as a stalking predator's beneath casual slacks and a fine woollen sweater. Having been taught by past experience to treat his rare periods of amiability as presentiments of danger, she broke into a nervous babble.

'Ponies that roam the hills and moors all during the summer are descendants of a breed that's been native to the islands for thousands of years, but to say that they're wild is as misleading as the popular theory that in winter they're forced to eat seaweed in order to survive. They all belong to somebody, and though owners' methods of looking after their stock vary, mares in foal are usually made comfortable in enclosures and the few that are left grazing during winter months are supplied with plenty of extra feed to supplement their sparse diet.'

Somehow, without apparent effort, Leon closed the gap between them. 'Cattle left to shift for themselves where feeding is sparse tend to be undersized and underdeveloped,' he mused. 'Perhaps if one were to try breeding Shetland ponies in a climate where the grazing is richer they would increase in height.'

Unwittingly duped into defending part of her islands' heritage, Catriona vigorously shook her head. 'No,' she corrected proudly, 'it's been proved conclusively that that's not the case—no matter where they live, no matter what they are fed, pure bred Shetland ponies retain their miniature proportions! How and when these uniquely small animals reached our islands is not known for certain, but during excavations of a Bronze Age settlement unearthed animal bones were examined and measured and found to compare very favourably with those of the existing Shetland pony. Viking invaders, who were known to have taken their stallions with them into battle, probably introduced another strain when they settled here, but during the years that have passed since their occupation the pony has gradually reverted to its original small size. Aunt Hanna kept a couple in the stables when I was a child,' she mused with a faintly nostalgic smile, 'it was always a blissfully happy day for me whenever, Citrine, my particular favourite, was not needed to cart fuel from the peat hill and I was allowed to use her as transport to take me to school.'

They had left the road far behind them, and as they sauntered over heather-covered moorland towards a coastline littered with reefs, stacks and skerries the smell of seaweed began mingling with the perfume of wild flowers being crushed beneath their feet, forming nature's own fragrant incense, a balm to soothe the senses and assuage the pain of savaged emotions.

Halting at the edge of cliffs dropping dramatically towards a stretch of sandy beach, Leon peered below, his attention riveted by a herd of chestnut, brown, black, grey, piebald and skewbald ponies with long, shaggy manes browsing among seaweed left stranded by an ebbing tide. When he leant forward to peer closer the air became suddenly animated by hundreds of pairs of beating wings as gannets, puffins, razorbills, guillemots and kittiwakes lifted from rocky perches to shriek raucous resentment of his presence. Hastily, he took a step backward when a piratical great skua rose into the air, then made a swooping dive in his direction.

'Look out!' she cautioned sharply, making a lunging grab for his arm when he seemed in danger of losing his balance. 'You must keep away from the edges of cliffs, they're often dangerously loose, especially after a spell of wet weather,' she scolded, shaken by his second close brush with danger.

When his glance quickened, his bright amber eyes questioning her shocked loss of colour, she snatched her hand from his arm, annoyed by the certainty that, to a man grown used to plumbing dangerous depths, her reaction must have appeared over-protective.

'I'm sorry, Kate, I seem fated to upset your serenity.' He did not sound mocking, nor even amused, just cautious as a hunter aware of a need to tread warily.

'You do . . .?' Though inwardly shaking, she strove to sound surprised, apparently unconcerned. 'I'm afraid I hadn't noticed.'

For a few tense seconds every angrily circling bird fell silent as if shocked by the lie. Then, heavily, Leon sighed.

'Let's sit for a while, Kate. I think it's time we had a serious talk, don't you?'

'What . . . what is there to talk about?' she stammered, alarmed by the insistent pressure of his hand upon her shoulder, levering her down upon the waterproof he had spread at her feet.

Dropping easily down beside her, he answered her question with a mild observation. 'Just lately, I've been moving more and more towards the conviction that people often reflect the character of their surroundings. You, for instance,' his head swung round to pin her startled face with sombre amber eyes, 'appear to possess affections that are as diverse as the Shetland landscape, one moment unyielding as granite and the next radiating the breathtaking appeal of hills emerging from the deep blue stillness of early morning. Then again, there are times when you betray the tough, hardy spirit of islanders reputed to have more salt than blood in their veins, and others when you seem as dignified and aloof as a Nordic snow princess.'

Catriona remained very still, her arms clasped around her knees, keenly sensitive to an atmosphere that had turned explosive—as if a sizzling fuse were about to ignite beneath his blanket of calm conversation.

'Unfortunately,' he confessed on a harsh note of apology, 'I, too, often reflect the character of my earlier surroundings—an ugly mining town offering no sense of continuity, inhabited mainly by a race of nomadic oilmen who regarded responsibility as a burden to be shifted as quickly as possible on to the shoulders of Destiny, Chance, Circumstance, or his nearest gullible neighbour.'

She stirred restlessly but did not interrupt when he dredged deeper to unearth what was obviously his most painful memory.

'During childhood days and early adolescence, my aunt was the only female influence in my life. She had many faults, but she was all I had and I loved her, Kate,' he admitted heavily. 'Consequently, I grew up using her as a criterion of womanhood, convinced that the ideal female was pretty but vain; flirtatious but flighty, prone to making ardent promises then breaking them without apology or remorse. Until you walked into my life,' his voice lowered to a depth of sincerity that caused her pulses to soar high as circling wings, 'I had no idea any other sort of girl existed—which was partly my own fault, I suppose, for as Geoff succinctly pointed out, one is hardly likely to meet a teetotaller in a drinking saloon.'

'You've spoken to Geoff?' Wincing from the reminder of an accusation branded heavily as shame upon her heart, she dared to swing round to face him. 'You didn't . . . you haven't . . .?'

Making no pretence of misunderstanding the plea directed by hurt green eyes, Leon slowly shook his head.

'No, thank goodness, I can still number Geoff among my friends—though only just,' he admitted wryly. 'You're the only person I've offended by voicing a suspicion which your shocked, stricken look immediately proved to be unfounded. I would have given my right arm for sufficient time to right the wrong I inflicted upon you that day, Kate,' he groaned, holding her eyes with a tortured look, yet making no move towards her. 'Lord knows, I didn't escape punishment, for a man locked away in solitary confinement finds plenty of time to meditate, to reflect upon his sins.'

In spite of the frenzied panic aroused by the sight of his fiery head lowering deliberately towards her, in spite of the fact that a nerve kicking in his cheek seemed to indicate that the arrogant oil boss was having great difficulty controlling a surging well of emotion, Catriona could not bite back a bitter retort.

'Am I hearing aright? Are you actually on the verge of admitting to an error, of conceding that you might possibly have been mistaken in your judgment of my morals?'

Much to the relief of nerves strained taut as elastic, Leon paused with his lips hovering a mere fraction away from hers as if to reassess his chances. When she refused to cower, continued to storm at him with her eyes, he condemned tightly,

'Dammit, Kate, must you fight me all the way? I've already apologised for my behaviour, but if you'd like me to, I'm even prepared to grovel! I'm sorry as hell to have hurt you; please try to forgive me, forget your Sheltie pride and surrender as only a woman can—without fear of defeat!'

Reminding herself of how often his sharp claws had remained sheathed—but waiting; how his eyes could convey gentleness, then suddenly revert to fire, she retaliated swiftly, before her traitorous body could bend beneath his will. Tilting a defiant chin, she accused with distaste,

'Understandably, an oil king can become accustomed to easy conquests during his black reign, but perhaps you might find it easier to understand my reluctance to become one of your subjects if I remind you that I belong to a race that's been repelling invaders for hundreds of years!'

When his head reared proudly she was reminded of the lion rampant worn like a talisman on his protective helmet. Then without warning he pounced, kissing her breathless as he forced her down among the heather, confirming her theory that she had been right to fight wary of being fooled by the mask of humility he had worn with unease, by refusing to believe that he was anything other than the hard, ruthless, impatient, domineering oil boss who had promised her a job for as long as he was kept amused by the novelty of taming a vixen, who had employed her as a decoy to distract attention from illicit affairs designed to break the monotony of his solitary rest days.

Behind a barrier of downcast lashes she fought hard against a languorous tide of longing; imposed the stillness of a statue upon a body crushed by hands seeking to arouse response, willed the chill of marble upon lips kissed to the keen glowing pink of wild thyme being tossed into a fragrant frenzy by a passing breeze.

She experienced no sense of triumph when, after a prolonged, sensuous onslaught he finally conceded defeat by lifting his mouth from hers to deride bitterly,

'You win, Mistress Kate! Clearly, you intend clinging to your bonnet of virtue until you're a "bittock" of thirty!'

She lay gasping, fighting to regain her breath and her scattered sanity, then braced before jumping to her feet to stagger backward until there was a yard of safe ground between herself and the temptation, growing stronger by the minute, to join the ranks of girls who had been wooed and then discarded by the man who had been careful to omit the word *love* from his extensive vocabulary.

Slowly he straightened, casting his dark, angry shadow over a trembling quarry whose piteous, tear-bright eyes were begging for compassion. For long-drawn-out seconds he returned her stare, fists clenching and unclenching as if desire were fighting a war with conscience, then as suddenly as a lamp being extinguished the flame in his amber eyes died, leaving them dark and deeply brooding.

'Don't look at me like that, Kate!' he jerked. 'If we can't share love, at least don't let us part in danger.'

'Love?' she choked, pushed to the brink of despair by this last sad play upon her emotions. 'I'd imagined you were a stranger to the word!'

She saw his tall frame jerk rigid, then had to harden her heart against what sounded almost like sincerity in his breathed accusation,

'How can you possibly doubt my love when for weeks I've been trying as hard as I know how to prove how much you mean to me? I admit that at first I was reluctant to put a name to an emotion so powerful it rendered me unable, for the first time ever, to concentrate my mind upon work; that pushed me to the verge of losing the respect of a valued friend through unreasonable jealousy. An emotion that filled me with despair and frustration when there appeared to be no hope of it ever being returned; that made me act savagely towards you when all I really wanted was to be gentle; made me ruthless instead of kind; forced me to rush impatiently when I knew how imperative it was to tread cautiously, one step at a time. It *must* be love I feel for you, Kate,' he groaned, 'either that, or I've gone suddenly and completely mad!'

'Leon!' She managed to gasp his name in spite of a tight throat, a heart beating powerfully as a great skua's wings. 'Oh, my poor love!'

She had managed to stumble no more than a couple of steps towards him before she was pulled hard against his chest, imprisoned within arms forming a tight band of possession that seemed determined never to let her go.

'Leon, my darling,' she whispered, lifting a shaking hand to stroke his temple where silver threads were lightly intermingled with dark russet red. 'If only you'd told me sooner! You must find the word love terribly hard to say!'

'I'll practise saying it to you every day for the rest of my life, Kate my love,' he promised huskily. Then with a return of the amber gleam that assured her that in spite of enjoying his role of humble subject the masterful king of the jungle was waiting in the wings, he growled softly against her inviting lips,

'But as it may take me quite some time to achieve a satisfactory standard of elocution, I'll continue communicating my love in the manner I know best—by constant and thorough demonstration!'

At first, he kissed her tenderly, gently, uncertainly as a thirsty traveller approaches a mirage, but when he discovered that she was real, urgently and sweetly responsive, he unleashed virile passion, drowning her in kisses, drawing her deeper and deeper into unexplored depths until she felt saturated with love, tossed by passionate currents, while lovingly, gradually, expertly, he initiated her into the heady, abandoned, delightful sensation known to lovers and divers alike as 'rapture of the deep' . . .

Harlequin® Plus

A WORD ABOUT THE AUTHOR

A small terrace house in northern England, overshadowed by the towering brick wall of a mill, with the frantic humming of looms forever in the background… This is the home of Margaret Rome, in which she spins love stories set in France, or in Italy, or on the banks of the Amazon.

Her first job was at a bakery, where her father, mother, sister and two brothers worked. She left there to be married and, after the birth of a son, took part-time work as an usherette, printer, waitress and shop assistant. Then came college, a teacher who inspired his writing class to reach new heights, and an announcement to her family one holiday weekend: "I think I'll write a book."

As good as her word, she completed her first manuscript in twelve weeks. Today, many romance novels later, Margaret Rome confesses that "it's still a thrill to see my name in print."

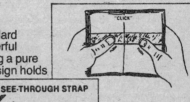

HARLEQUIN CLASSIC LIBRARY

Great old romance classics from our
early publishing lists.

FREE
BONUS
BOOK

On the following page is a coupon with which
you may order any or all of these titles. If you
order all nine, you will receive a FREE book –
Doctor Bill, a heartwarming classic romance
by Lucy Agnes Hancock.

The thirteenth set
of nine novels in the
HARLEQUIN CLASSIC LIBRARY

Great old favorites...
Harlequin Classic Library

Complete and mail this coupon today!

Harlequin Reader Service

In U.S.A.
1440 South Priest Drive
Tempe, AZ 85281

In Canada
649 Ontario Street
Stratford, Ontario N5A 6W2

Please send me the following novels from the Harlequin Classic Library. I am enclosing my check or money order for $1.50 for each novel ordered, plus 75¢ to cover postage and handling. If I order all nine titles at one time, I will receive a FREE book, *Doctor Bill,* by Lucy Agnes Hancock.

☐ 109 ☐ 112 ☐ 115
☐ 110 ☐ 113 ☐ 116
☐ 111 ☐ 114 ☐ 117

Number of novels checked @ $1.50 each = $_____

N.Y. and Ariz. residents add appropriate sales tax $_____

Postage and handling $_____.75

TOTAL $_____

I enclose _____
(Please send check or money order. We cannot be responsible for cash sent through the mail.)
Prices subject to change without notice.

Name _____
(Please Print)

Address _____
(Apt. no.)

City _____

State/Prov. _____

Zip/Postal Code _____

Offer expires December 31, 1983.   30656000000